BEYOND OBLIVION

by

Kim Kacoroski

Cover art illustrations by Kim Kacoroski, Phillipe Velasquez, and Masha Tatarintsev

Visit the author website:
http://kimkacoroski.com

ISBN: 978-1-947036-01-7 (Paperback)

Version 2019.5.9

Book Two of the Oblivion Series

Beyond Oblivion

Other Books in the Oblivion Series

Escape from Oblivion I

Oblivion's Edge III

Oblivion's Deal IV

Flight from Oblivion V

Books in Flight Series

Flight from Oblivion I

Eagle's Flight in the American Revolution II

Flight of the Ascendants in the American Revolution III

Choices from the American Revolution IV

Bridges of Flight before the American Revolution V

Testimony VI

Books in the Camelon Series

The Promise of Camelon I

The Dragons of Camelon II

History of the World According to the Druids III

New Beginnings IV

Kingdom of the Golden Tara V

Bridges of Flight before the American Revolution VI

INTRODUCTION

BEYOND OBLIVION recovers a generation. America remembers the Sixties Generation by its music, whereas the Eighties remained silent in comparison. The Eighties Generation appreciated music as a gift, despite the violent growth of technology that permeated private, dead-air spaces. This younger generation voted with their feet, and left places that insulted their ears. They found their freedom by making choices in airspace; the Eighties generation defined themselves by the boundaries that they kept and learned to tune out.

Compared to the cacophony of the Sixties, the Eighties became a time of love songs with heart-wrenching notes and soft, reflective melodies. In a tarot deck, the Lovers' card represents the path of love, the freedom in being able to make choices in life. Love seeks completeness and wholeness, a blissful reconciliation involving both sides of the brain. Fools and magicians seldom follow their passions, an emotional realm far removed from the habitations of stars, sun, moon, and planets. Those seeking justice or balance often find a loveless trail. The Eighties generation sought relief from the confusion by listening to amorous melodies.

Intending to have this book be heard as well as read, my comment has been provided with the background music of the Eighties. For the sake of clarity, a few contemporary tunes lace the chapters. The task of finding the words to the residual melodies remains to the reader. Sometimes wrong, sometimes right, the subtleties of these songs serve as an interface between the world's dictations and private affairs. Echoes in a concrete canyon fade, whereas the resonant tunes of love endure. Caught between the ages of world wars and computerized disconnection, the Eighties Generation thrived and freed itself. There will be no other generation like it.

Chapter One

Tune Reference: Father and Son

----Cat Stevens

ON A DARK and stormy afternoon, Donna took a particular fork in the road. She raced across campus in the shower as lightning streaked across the gray clouds. A swirl of red, yellow, and orange leaves dotted her path over the brick mall. Careful to avoid slipping in the torrent, she thought about recent world events affecting the atmosphere on the small college campus. Earlier this December, John Lennon had been shot, and he seemed to disappear out of the American peace scene with his song *Imagine*. His absence jarred young people into asking questions, which seemed a rational response in a world that seemed irrational. In the last interview with Rolling Stone magazine, Lennon and Yoko admitted to having been used by the industry they helped create.

Oblivious to the reasons behind the present whirlwind of world events, Donna slid into the chair facing the silver-haired Hungarian monk, the one known as the 'White Tiger.' Being the only female student in the physics department that he chaired, she began questioning the Rome experience, a curriculum designed for graduates intending to study abroad. In Rome, she planned to take a few courses relevant to her studies in geology. Smiling faintly at her as she stood in the doorway, he waved for her to enter and sit down near his desk. Unlike the others, she cultivated the sensitivity and awareness, which earned her a reputation as being bright. Momentarily he paused to stare at the student as if weighing how much time he wanted to spend talking to her. Tapping his fingers together in mild delight, he conveyed admiration in the way that she looked into a theoretical physics derivation and thought it through to the end. Realizing that she had other questions on her mind besides physics, he leaned back in his chair with a frown. Unfortunately, this inclination carried over into the way she approached her life.

"I have this feeling that the Pope John Paul II is in danger," she started, while shaking her head over her books. Her feelings about the risk of travel in a foreign country contrasted with the expectations of the academics. For similar reasons, she had never been a Beatles fan, having sensed that they sold out after *Yesterday*. She didn't want an imaginary world that Lennon creation, instead Donna preferred a real one and sought the monk's advice. Graduate students had told her about a Padre with the stigmata, a wound that some called sacred, whereas others considered the injury as imaginary. The older classmates sensed an association with the Padre's convent and underworld. With a laugh, they tossed off the tensions surfacing in Eastern Europe. Explaining her concerns to the physicist-monk, she felt him out. "They say he has the stigmata. It seems that tensions are surfacing all over Eastern Europe. Is it all part of the Communist threat? People still struggle for freedom."

She watched him closely. The White Tiger had earned his name by crawling away to freedom when communists took over his monastery in

Hungary. Bullets had whizzed past his head and some priests had been left behind.

He beamed at her for a few moments as if she had solved one of life's major riddles. Realizing that she had succeeded in arousing his interest, she pressed him further for a thoughtful answer from a greater authority on world affairs than her sophomoric classmates. As she groped for an answer, Donna imagined seeing a Santa Dragon sitting at his desk. This magical dragon could fly and protect its riders. She called the dragon 'Santa' because the rider looked like a gnome. Finally, she understood what made the White Tiger tick.

"There is a lot going on in the world. It's hard to just sit back and study," she confessed. Founded with the help of a well-known right-wing, CIA asset, her classmates often joked about signing up for the army as a way to pay their way through medical school. 'Kill a commie for mommie' became their motto. School officials pressured those on campus to investigate international affairs in the manner that other young adults experimented with drugs and sex. She knew one student who had been deported for climbing the Vatican wall. Another talked about how he had flushed eastern European currency down the toilet in a train before inspectors arrived. Donna questioned whether she would be safe in her academic pursuits overseas.

He turned from her and faced the paperwork on his desk. Briefly, he appeared to be consulting the imaginary gnome, which served as his muse for the moment. In physics class, she had learned how to see beyond light particles, calculate other dimensions, and define the invisible.

"Stay out of it," he softly said.

She detected an edge in his tone, and fathomed the truth of his words. He had presented her with an alternative reality, one that eluded the Greek goddesses of fates, who not only wove the threads of people's lives, but cut them decisively. This priest encouraged her to cut loose from foolhardy destinies by setting a limit on the integration abroad.

Then he faced her as he added, "The best thing you can do for the world is to be happy. Get married. Enjoy your family."

Dumbfounded, she realized that he didn't refer to the families he had known in the old country. Though he represented the most intelligent, joyful person she knew over the age of sixty-five, his view of her generation in America appeared naive. Somehow, the simple isolated world of the American family stirred the imagination of the White Tiger. Having educated her without a hint of regret for his own celibacy, he observed the American family as a magical phenomenon. Donna never said another word, leaving him alone in his fantasy. Her childhood moments had subsisted on a steady diet of Hardy Boys and Nancy Drew books interlaced with *Scooby Doo* cartoon mysteries and *Partridge Family* music. In the summer evenings, she and her enterprising teen friends voiced occasional whispers about the biggest mystery of all, less than a ten-minute drive on the other side of the nearby professional football stadium. She simply nodded as she recalled going to the mysterious assassination site in Dallas as an excursion for a ten-year-old birthday party. Many of her friends had fathers in the military and lived with the realization that their father could be gunned down at any moment as well. Protected by a fully armed motorcade, this dad had perished on the streets while others stood by. No one had returned the fire. The only explanation came in the form of a tiny museum near the old warehouses. As cars raced down the street as if nothing had occurred, Donna and her friends briefly studied the supposed trajectories for the assassin's bullet. Now, after having passed first year physics, she still had not been convinced that anyone, even a lone nut, could make the shot from the depository building and do such damage.

The mystery remained as to why no one had voiced disagreement with the summary presented in the museum. Her cohorts agreed that it would be better to address their questions in a slumber party seance than pursue the mystery in the physical world. Though the notion initially captivated the imagination of those gathered for the sleepover, the enthusiasm diminished quickly as her friends realized that the shot had served as a warning. For this reason, Donna hesitated to venture to another city halfway around the world, romanticized with blood-soaked, fallen coliseums. Television images touted Rome as the city of love, but like other things in life, Donna dismissed the notion as another lie. Celibacy and martyrdom provided Rome's distinction in physical reality.

Walking down the shiny, polished floors of the empty corridor into the haze of the dimly-lit entry hall, Donna thought about her revelation. Something about it insulated her from the tensions on campus, where the students perceived world affairs only through the intellect. Though marriage had not occurred to her, the lure of overseas graduate study and travel suddenly lost its appeal, even for the sake of nostalgia. The monk's advice mirrored her gut feelings, though he took a harder line and seeded the idea to forego the risky excursion. Within six months, there would be assassination attempts on Pope John Paul II as well as President Reagan.

Donna opened the glass doors of the building and exited the physics building. Stepping into the bright sunlight, she felt as if she was leaving it all behind her. The bricked pavement on the mall stretched in front of her like an ancient Roman highway. Not all roads led to Rome; she persevered to take the road less traumatized.

She waved off a mutual acquaintance, heralding pamphlets concerning the Priory of Sion and heading straight for her. This student had earned Padre Pio's ire during her studies in Italy. Though the woman and her friends had never said anything, the Padre called them disbelievers and chased them away. For a priest who supposedly carried the stigmata, he seemed fairly touchy. Donna wondered how he could doubt the belief of anyone who passed out Society of the Rose pamphlets almost religiously.

"Friends do not give friends stigmatas," Donna remarked when she heard the anecdotal story from several fellow classmates.

The story served as part of the campus puzzle like a brick in the mall leading to Rome. There were so many anecdotes to fathom. She knew that the head of the philosophy department had smuggled Nazis out of Spain during WWII. Classmates loved retelling tales about his stunts over beers at the campus cafe.

"Which side was he playing?" a young man asked, after he stopped gabbing with the others at her table.

"He claims to be Opus Dei, something for the church."

"Oh, that explains it," someone else reasoned. "What is Opus Dei?"

"Nobody knows," a third person added. "They are all sworn to secrecy."

"Well, the chair of the English department is a die-hard Confederate," an eavesdropper retorted. "It always helps to know the background of the professors who grade our compositions."

"Didn't they lose the war?" a bystander joked.

"What do ya mean? He and his colleagues go to all the conventions," the bystander's companion mused.

"Red rover, red rover, let's get Maximillan to come over..." a history major stated with a whimsical air.

"Maximillan was a Hapsburg ruler planted in Mexico during the Civil War. The Hapsburgs ruled the Holy Roman Empire for 900 years," a political science major told them.

"Hey, is this what happens when history majors and political scientists drink beer with geologists?" Donna asked with a twinkle in her eye. Keeping the conversation light before another crusade broke out, she sidestepped these heavy thought-provoking conversations that were a campus trademark. The editor of the school newspaper had just penned an article entitled "How I Learned the Lively Art of Schmoozing."

"Don't forget the Mises Institute. The chair of the Business and Economics Department is a sworn Mises guy," an economics grad student rejoined, after having overheard the conversation from the nearby table.

"More beer!" the political science grad announced. Rising to his feet, he explained, "I've hit my limit concerning information overload. "Who cares! Immortals like Nicholas Hapsberg run the show. Some say that he is a vampire. The family intermarried with the Cup of Borgia and Vlad the Impaler during the Crusades."

"Here's to the Fates that weave the destinies of our lives!" another shouted. "The Austrian financial wizards are in league with them."

"Cheers to more Hapsburg derived institutions!" the history graduate hailed, raising his mug. "Now how many chairs in the Federal Reserve studied with Mises?"

"If it wasn't for the Russian blockade, the South would have been back into the Holy Roman Empire. Bye, bye Romanovs," the history major interjected. "Thousands of people wanted to kill Lincoln. The Vatican became an inconspicuous no-show at the funeral. According to White House records, the Austrian Hapsburg ruler slapped Lincoln on the face with his white gloves for not accepting his royal loan---the ballroom party of the century!"

"Oh, no way," Donna said, waving her hand in front of her face as if to ward off more revelations. "You're too much."

"That is how we keep our sanity during the studies, otherwise the stuff gets incredibly boring and canned. We just find out the truth on the side—it is much more interesting. Who cares about investigating political smears when you get all this to rake through?" The history graduate looked down at the table and paused for a moment. Glancing at the group gathered around him, he asked, "Want another beer?"

"Remember the Greenbacks?" the political science major quizzed them. Nobody on campus ever dropped an intense political, historical, philosophical discussion concerning economics. "The dictators started calling the president a dictator, though Jefferson actually had intended the nation to make its own money. Lincoln wasn't out of line."

"Economic transference," a psychology graduate piped from the same table as the economics graduate.

"Oh you're bad," the history graduate said as he playfully slapped the economics major.

"Okay, I'm out," Donna announced as she rose from the table.

Walking away from the din, she considered her own limits. Crossing her arms over her jacket, she blocked out any more heart-felt engagements. A few yards away from the gathering, she reached inside the jacket of her pocket to palm one of her favorite rocks. There were significant reasons why she studied rocks and none of these other disciplines. Rocks had the historical record etched in them. Their history wasn't left for fleeting revelations over beer in a campus cafe. As she raced across the brick mall, Donna examined the bordering wooded area for signs of life. With a nod, she noted the sudden absence of vitality in the undergrowth, a dramatic change from the previous day. Something had shifted for the worse. No magic in the leaves or underbrush. The forest seemed dead. No hint of interdimensional beings from the MidEarth. All the nature spirits had vanished into an alternative reality. Donna pondered these implications, which cued her to leave this campus behind. Taking the fork in the road had led her to another place, a destination separate from the present university. Armed with these observations, she disappeared from the coordinates defining her previous existence, as if finding a portal to another world, or a change in scenery.

Chapter Two

Truth entertains a value

Rather than a mood

Tune Reference: *Nights in White Satin*

----The Moody Blues

THE NEXT WEEK Donna met with the campus priest.

"I want the Last Rites," she told him. Having seen him trance out during meditations in church, Donna sensed that he would comply with her demand. Although most reserved the Last Rites for the dying, Donna resonated with the White Tiger's advice to avoid religion and politics. It would be one way to blow off those who felt that they owned all the sheep in the fold. She didn't want to be herded like a sheep any longer. Donna yearned for a spiritual life that made sense to her.

"OK," he said, staring into space. "Must be a spiritual death."

Shaking her head lightly, Donna focused on the books in front of her without saying a word.

"Come back next week," he advised her.

Donna nodded her head silently in agreement. She studied the tiled floor beneath her feet for signs of a firm foundation. The unleveled surface indicated that she wouldn't be able to find such terrain. After leaving quickly, she walked back across the mall bricks towards her apartment off campus.

In the middle of the mall, another mutual acquaintance approached her with a pamphlet for Young Republicans. She roomed with the woman who speared-headed the organization, which seemed to be catching on like wildfire on a campus marred by student apathy. Donna shook her head. The president of the school's student government had won on the 'Vote for Bill, He Doesn't Care' platform. After passing on the propaganda, Donna collected her thoughts. She surmised that the opposite of love was not hate, but apathy. In another time, she suspected that MLK would have been a member of the local Petroleum Club and presented his daughter in debutante balls if given half a chance. Always one for appearances, MLK noted how many times the pallbearers dropped JFK's casket. Such national subtleties were enough to discourage any heartfelt high school debater from entering politics at any level. At this point in her life, Donna sensed that the issues extended beyond her.

She did not have anything against ballroom dances, Democrats, Republicans, and Petroleum, after accidentally crashing one of the ballroom dances of the Young Sophisticates. In silent protest of the emerging campus establishment, the same young man who had been deported for climbing the Vatican wall had showed up late for his date. Donna had learned that his date had been the woman with the Young Republican pamphlets. The deportee had arrived slightly drunk, barefoot, attired in nothing but blue jeans and a checkered shirt. Sometime, during the elite party, Donna had entered the forbidden-zone to deliver a message to the same woman with the pamphlets. Though Donna arrived dressed in her favorite corduroy-painter's pants and a flannel shirt, a tuxedo-clad young man asked Donna to dance and whisked her around the dance floor. Her friend, Carrie, had introduced him to Donna as one of her physics lab instructors. Other tuxedo-clad men stepped in as the women in formal dress watched and seemed more bored than irritated. Meanwhile, the woman who founded the Young Republicans and Young Sophisticates still had not forgiven Donna for stopping her well-aimed attempt to score a last minute soccer goal at the game lost week. Fortunately, the woman became obsessed with transforming Dallas into either New York City or a Virginia plantation, and buried the grudge. Donna had never been to New York City, Virginia, played soccer, or waltzed until this year. She remained bipartisan for the upcoming election, while discovering that she relished ballroom dancing with enthusiastic partners.

When the Vatican deportee stepped in, they gracefully floated across the ballroom floor for the duration of the evening. Donna could appreciate a young man with a Jesuit education, where they learned how to formally dance with women. She knew from her experiences as a retreat counselor that the school administrators made ballroom dancing a requirement at the all-boys high school. Unlike many of the others at the dance, the Vatican deportee was a local boy and grounded in his cowboy ways. Like the miraculous game-saving soccer catch, many of the onlookers found the couple amusing, if not inspiring.

"You know, they think that Reagan is the leader in Revelations—-the one who is going to head us into Armageddon," she had overheard her housemate tell Carrie the other day. "He has the star of David in his astrology chart or something like that. They think he is the one."

Her housemate, the daughter of LBJ's private pilot, dated Donna's childhood friend. Having lost his soul somewhere between grade school and college, their relationship never regained its warmth in college. A descendant of the Irish Collas tribe, he now sat out all the dances and did nothing but study. Carrie, another one of Donna's childhood friends, had a boyfriend who also was related to the same Collas tribe. His Collas ancestor had not only signed the Declaration of Independence, but had moved the national capitol from Philadelphia to the District of Columbia. The districts around the university campus bore the name Los Colinas, which reflected the power of this ruling class.

Donna sighed and eventually accepted the pamphlet like another brick in the pavement. What did it all mean? Who was behind all this? Despite the preface in Revelations condemning anyone who came up with an interpretation, the undergraduates were required to develop their own. She had heard several versions of Revelations, usually at schmoozes like the one she had just left. An english major had noted that the preface to Revelations was very similar to Mark Twain's preface in *Innocents Abroad*, where he condemned anyone who tried to make sense out of his story. Now a scholarly interpretation of Revelations became a class requirement. Who else but the academics would care about delving into such negativity? For Donna, the class assignment had been like quicksand, once a scholar landed in the mess, they could not easily get out of it. The issues shifted endlessly, unless you were on firm ground with the professor.

Donna waved off the acquaintance and resumed her walk. If Reagan ran on the Armageddon platform, then a vote for him would be a choice for Armageddon. Could a person choose Armageddon like choosing to have the Last Rites? Could the population vote on it? Would her personal choice count? Donna wanted to write her own script on the end of the world. She had her feet on the ground regarding that issue. No one had ever considered the notion that Armageddon had already come and gone, like the thief in the night or something like that. Donna found enough pain in the planet's historical record to create the second coming and then some.

"Yah, they claimed that Lincoln was a fallen away Catholic," Donna overheard two other graduates engage each other on a nearby bench.

"That's what the Cathars said about all the Protestants," one acquaintance retorted. Donna stared at the man, who attended the Lutheran church off campus. She noticed that none of the Catholics protested.

"Well, that's what they get for starting the Inquisition."

"What? Do you want to discuss this over a bottle of wine? Who started the Inquisition?"

Donna walked briskly by the casual debate.

"They groomed Lincoln for the presidency," another insisted. "One prof claimed that the daughter of a London banker had him out of wedlock."

"Do you mean that honest Abe was a love child?" a member of a study group asked.

"Maybe that is why they poisoned his mother," the other student answered. "Imagine growing up with that knowledge. Of course, honest Abe turned the tables on the bankers."

"You're right," her companion added. "My research indicates that only two of the signers of the Declaration of Independence were not financed by the Bank of England."

"That's history for you," the second student agreed. "We'll have to erase most of the faces on Mount Rushmore and reprint our money. Remove the Serpentine occult symbolism on our bills and revert Truman's flag." He bounced nervously on his feet as he fathomed the intrigue. He reasoned, "Truman pulled a fast one there. The symbols are consistent with the decision to nuke Japan after the war was almost over. Consider it a decision by the corporate oligarchs, the ones who owned University of Chicago, Einstein, General Electric, and the nuclear industry."

Then the conversation shifted to a slightly different note. One young man proposed, "Then there is the Dauphin of France from Valois, another ruler from the House of Capet and Serpentine agenda. The Dauphin fooled Joan of Arc, Napoleon's heroine."

"Hegel, Hegel," a nearby voice murmured. "It's the Serpentine dialectic that you gotta know for the test tomorrow," a young man instructed a study group sequestered on another bench on the mall.

"The Hegelian dialectic?" a dazed student murmured. "Yin and Yang? Are they considered equal and opposite reactions, like Newton's financiers?"

"Sorta, but the Serpentines funded the dynamic where both sides are played against each other, like the European bankers did during the Napoleon invasion," another student chimed. Then he scratched his head as he muttered, "They funded Hegel too. By the way, Napoleon's second wife was a Hapsburg."

"Equal and opposite. That's Newton's mechanical universe. Was he paid, too?"

"By the British crown."

"Who owned them?"

"The bankers, the ones who owned the shipping company at the Boston Tea Party and financed most of signers of the Declaration of Independence, not to mention Hamilton and his bank. The Patriots dumped tea and opium from their boats." The young man paused and thumped his chest firmly. He glanced at his buddies standing near him and smiled in jest.

Another slaphappy student nudged the man before he could speak further. He announced, "I am going to party hard after finals."

"What! We can't put that down on the test. You gotta know the professors. They'll kill us!" a nearby group of sleep-deprived, anxious students shrieked.

"I still gotta do my essay on *The Wasteland*," another panicked.

"Do you think T. S. Eliot was wasted when he did that one?" the dazed student pondered.

"What a waste," one of the anxious students groaned.

Realizing why history repeated itself, Donna gazed at the phallic bell-tower at the far end of the mall. Every hour, chimes rang from the top of the obelisk and marked the passage of time for the students below. She picked up her pace, feeling relieved that she had completed finals last week.

The next week she met with the priest and obtained the Last Rites without any fanfare. The discussions that she had overheard on campus convinced her of the wisdom in demanding a sacramental death rather than becoming a cursed, fallen away Catholic. Donna did not want to be on the same list as Lincoln, preferring to learn from his mistake. She continued to finish the last details on her thesis and plot her career change.

At the end of the week something unexpected happened. The priest called her and compelled her to meet the head of the Psychology department. For some reason, he suddenly had reservations about giving out the Last Rites before the individual died. Donna agreed with his viewpoint and consented with some reservation. Naively curious and slightly dazed from the heavy curriculum, she never foresaw the entrapment.

Donna entered the large meeting room and accepted the priest's invitation to sit down near the psychology professor. Pushing aside her sense of betrayal, she observed the priest's ally in the apparent breach of confidential information. She recalled the words of her former boyfriend,

Charlie, who had complained about the crazy department chair during romantic interludes. Charlie referred to the campus as *The Wasteland,* and eventually Donna dropped him when his drinking became excessive. The academic culture affected him deeply, whereas Donna found intellectual debates entertaining. Though Charlie remained emotionally unavailable, Donna valued his insight and reason. He had been her lover and she could not forget him. The things Charlie said, the way he said them, and the way he loved her, stayed with her. Reminiscences of Charlie made her present dealings with the academics more poignant. Having gone on a personal mission to find himself, Charlie protected her with the searing memory of those long, deep kisses that went on for hours.

Other classmates simply enlisted, opting for what they considered an inexpensive route through medical school. With the looming war in the gulf, Donna shuddered at the thought of her former classmates fighting it out in the sands of the Mideast, which would be surely loaded with toxic chemicals in this day and age. She did not consider it much of a future. This option seemed comparable to going to the Texas gulf coast for a vacation and swimming around all the oil derricks that had almost sprung up overnight, just as she had done last year. Tar balls from the mess clung to skin and bathing suits, unless vacationers swam fast or became slippery. The owner of all the wells had gone bankrupt, so there was no money to pay for cleanups, much less eyesores. Much worse, word was out that he had his sights on the US presidency. Donna longed for the return of a simpler world, where an individual did not see an oil-soaked horizon. She realized that she would have to work hard to keep the corporate world from dictating her perspective.

"They say you are a mystic," the psychology chair confronted.

Donna frowned. She considered herself a geologist, a professional in the science of grounded observation. The professor ruminated as the priest remained silent. She cocked her head to the side and studied the man, as if trying to figure out the basis for his anger.

"You are a scared little girl inside," he suddenly accused her.

Donna blinked and took a step back as her unfailing sense of humor stepped in. Finding his statement absurd, she looked at him quizzically. She realized that she had stepped out of the box, the one containing all the frightened students cramming for tests between drinking bouts. Clinging to this sense of proportion during the conversation, she remained silent.

"I want you to stay here with me until you are safe," he continued as if hypnotizing her or something. Apparently, he had not heard of her career change. She had already decided to drop her studies in Europe.

"No, I have other plans," Donna politely replied, with a slight hint of irritation at his incestuous offer. Wondering whether it was just some cheap parlor trick to endlessly exploit a grad student, she decisively sidestepped his proposal. "I'm almost done here."

A knock interrupted the man's tirade and the priest went to the door to retrieve a note from the secretary. He handed the note to the professor, who rushed out of the room to take the phone call.

"His mother had a heart attack," the priest explained as he dismissed Donna from the room.

Stunned by the reprieve, she thought, *at least someone in his family has a sense of ethics. This man could break any mother's heart.* Glancing at the harsh black lines interrupting the reddish-brown wood panels on the wall, Donna merely accepted the announcement as a cruel jest and hurried underneath the illumined exit sign at the end of the huge office. Shaking her head in the cool breeze outside the building, she freed herself from the insanity permeating the university. Donna walked briskly past the campus shadows and thought about the abuse. *Why beat up a dead Catholic?* She straightened her back as she considered the adage, *dead Catholics don't lie, even if they are Welsh like Lincoln.*

Chapter Three

Daydreams of you

And your love

Lighten my load

Tune Reference: *Wishing You Were Here*

----Chicago

DURING THE FOLLOWING week, the priest pressured Donna to meet with the head of the sociology department. He made it clear that his supervisors would pursue her, if she didn't comply with their demands. This time she decided to take the initiative and soften the encounter. She handed the sociology professor a small figure of a horse as he welcomed her into his office. This time the priest bailed out of the meeting.

He looked at the figurine and gasped, "This is the symbol for a project that I have been working on. Nobody here knows about it."

Accepting the horse, he fingered it between his two hands. "This is crazy," he muttered.

He motioned her inside the office and offered her a chair by the sun-streaked window opposite his desk. The rows of books and mounds of papers strewn across the entire office indicated that he had no time to waste on inquisitions or witch hunts. He sat down on his desk chair and leaned back. His eyes stared at half of the ceiling as he looked at Donna out of politeness more than interest. Though he seemed lost for words, the professor began to lightly chat about her academic plans.

Donna accepted his chatty conversation without interruption as her glance followed his absent stare. Like two actors compelled to do a scene that held no interest for either of them, the discussion reached glib proportions. She offered pat responses to his generalized questions. Then he showed her the door, a gesture which won Donna's expression of sincere appreciation.

Donna wondered what Charlie would have said about her interaction with the sociology professor. A year older, he forewarned her about the academic insanity reaching epidemic proportions on campus. Compared to other people that she knew, their relationship had never been consummated. Neither wanted to commit, fulfilled by the intensity of their moments together. Anything more would have blown them apart, and they did not hunger for the next thrill. In light of the campus environment, their attraction seemed to be one of mutual preservation. All their kissing had only led to more intimate discussions about life and philosophy, which proved useful as Donna stripped the illusions from her present circumstances. In some ways, it appeared as if their relationship had not ended. They had merely chosen different paths. He turned to programming and alcohol, while she went on to confront and assert herself on the concerns that had once defined them as a couple. Now she felt alone without someone to check her reality or be her confidant. Left with the passion that Charlie had aroused, Donna acknowledged her metaphorical baby.

She rose, shook his hand, and went past him as he opened the door of his office to the outside world. "This is crazy," she overheard him mutter under his breath, a second time.

She merely turned to face him when she reached the hall. Hurrying to exit this scene, she nodded and left. Memories of Charlie faded into the walls on campus. As she left the building for the outdoors, Donna quit blaming Charlie. Her penchant for political angles had started with Duke, her first date, who had been Student Council President of the major high school in Tyler, Texas. In high school, she had run teenage retreats at area churches and harbored familiarity with the superficial culture of area high schools. The educational system promoted football and fast sport cars between wet and dry towns. A wet town sold alcohol, whereas a dry town prohibited such a beverage. She had met Duke while splashing with debate partners and roommates in the Fort Worth water gardens. Driven outdoors by the summer heat, they finished the college-debate workshop early and looked for water. Obviously lit by the exchange of ideas and thought-provoking discussion, the swimmers temporarily quenched their thirst. Frolicking in one of the pools where the movie producers had filmed a scene in *Logan's Run*, they all entered a whole new world of love, light, and logic. When Donna returned alone with Duke to the water gardens later, she asked him to not kiss her, asserting that she wasn't ready and didn't want to get in too deep in a relationship that would end as soon as it began. With a soft smile, the young senior acquiesced and honored her request as a sophomore. Instead, the couple settled in each other's arms as they talked of future goals and student governing bodies, while falling in love more deeply than they ever knew.

Entering high school after the summer, she dated her debate partner, a senior with a greater perspective on the world. Howard took her on long evening car rides to discuss case strategies. Together they solved the world problems, sometimes driving halfway to San Antonio on Highway 281. One midnight they rode the tram connecting airlines at DFW, where they contemplated health care at the national level. This came after they drove to Dallas to ride the elevator in a hotel that had the shape of a glass golf ball. They explored the notion of a federal ban on tobacco, which eventually became a winning case in several tournaments. Two years later, she went to the same golf-ball hotel for her senior prom, while Howard set up the debate program at Columbia University where he had a scholarship. For the prom, Donna dated the State Champion wrestler and wound up back at the water gardens with their double-dates. Fort Worth had prohibited swimming in the public water gardens by the time of her senior prom. After an affectionate walk in the moonlight, everyone decided to catch the last fifteen minutes of a grade-B horror movie in the wee hours of the morning. After some Chinese fire drills and California rolls in the mall parking lot, they were forced to enter the back door of the movie theater where the audience greeted them with applause. The ticket box told them that they had shut down for the night and would not accept money from roaming prommers.

Friends made at the water gardens laced her high school days. Somehow, their rival high school had managed to attract the National Student Council Conference the summer before her junior year. One young adult presenter from Boston asked Donna if he could accompany her to the dance on the last night. An African American friend from the debate found at the water gardens, served as president of a big Fort Worth high school student council, and became a fierce rival on the high school debate circuit. He joined them, and the three of them shut out the world on the dance floor. Sherman, her friendly debate rival had been one of Duke's chums at the water garden swim. Something about uninhibitedly splashing with a debater in public water fountains bonded a person for life. Though she never saw Duke again, she ran into Sherman everywhere for the next three years. When the dance ended, Sherman warmly kissed her good-bye and politely dropped out, until the next high school debate. The boy from Boston escorted her to the buses, where he memorably kissed Donna in front of all the other high school councils in the nation.

As she briskly roamed past the scrub brush, yellow grass, and oak trees that lined the brick mall, Donna recalled the wisdom of her class yell. "WE RAISE HELL AND HAVE A GOOD TIME, SENIOR '79." Though it had been several years since being surrounded by such company, she could never forget such teenage contracts. The contrast shone through the darkness of the university where only the illumined sons and daughters of the moneyed-establishment thrived. Donna had her own history, certain of the joy and fun to be had in the world beyond.

When Donna reached her apartment a mile away from the professor's office, she began packing her things. Whatever had forced the sociology chair to spend time with her in idle amiable chatter must have a huge amount of clout. She could sense a network of forces at play like the numerous poisonous tentacles on a beached jellyfish. Beachcombers went out of their way to avoid stepping on the almost invisible appendages, often cutting a wide angle in the trajectory of their casual walk.

Donna could tell she that campus academics had singled her out, but couldn't figure out why. Being a cheerful morning-person on a campus where many nursed perpetual morning hangovers, Donna learned to cultivate a low profile. Never imbibing at Ground Hog's Day bonfires, she enjoyed the polkas. Though she kept her happiness to herself, sometimes her spirit just effervesced like champagne from a freshly uncorked bottle. Donna knew that she had inadvertently irritated the chronically-drunk daughter of a celebrated heart surgeon, one who operated the campus cathouse with her roommate.

Again, maybe this particular class of people nourished a grudge because Donna and her buddies had whopped them in a volleyball match. Her motley team played a game attune to quantum volleyball, while this group remained stuck in brutality and lost as a result. Despite their terror-driven ways, the perpetrators became easily intimidated.

Nothing compared to obtaining information from first-hand sources, and Donna educated herself in the political atmosphere. Carrie's Collas boyfriend had a relative that came from the same Polish town and had the same maiden name as Pope John Paul II. Unlike the pope, this relation had fled to Canada and burned all reminders, claiming that Poland no longer represented the home that she once knew. Obviously this man's grandmother had different values, whatever they were, in a land seized by Nazis fascists. Faced with the same terror-driven tactics on campus, Donna clung to her values along with the insights entertained with Charlie.

Donna dialed the number for the ticket agent at the regional airport and quickly altered her scheduled departure. Though she had changed her graduation plans, she had yet to change her airline reservation. She had been considering backpacking in Europe rather than pursuing intense study. Now she decided against travel abroad, which put Europe completely out of the picture. Her instincts told her that she needed to surround herself with a friendly crowd and remain visibly protected—in this country, which many considered to be home of the brave and land of the free. These ideals contrasted with the terrain of the university, which boasted funding branded with faraway names like Constantine. The university foundation sported real estate owners such as Bobby Baker and Greater Southwest Corporation, another LBJ association. She did not have anything against Greater Southwest Corporation per se. The corporation also owned the amusement park where she and her childhood Collas friend had once frequented. Many of her high school friends found jobs there during the summer. Cradling the phone in her lap, Donna sighed and realized that she had gained a valuable education at the university. With such knowledge, came responsibility, especially regarding lifestyle choices.

At the very least, Donna decided that now was the time for a long overdue vacation. Rather than return home and draw attention to her parents, she opted to hang out near a favorite family vacation spot just a few hours south of Boston. Quickly, she gathered her things and left a note for her roommates, none of whom she knew well enough to trust. People came and went without explanation in the university's shared housing. Her roommates knew she planned to leave soon; a quick note and an abrupt departure were not out of the ordinary in this superficial culture, though it really wasn't her style. She figured she could always plead 'family emergency,' if pressed for more information. She owed an explanation to only two people, who planned to travel with her and attend undergraduate classes on the Rome campus. Under the circumstances, Carrie and Jerome would have to make their journey to Italy without her. They would wonder what had happened to her, but she could get a note to them. When dealing with the shadows emanating from an illumined terrain, one's path in life never evolved straightforwardly or as expected. Instead, it became serpentine, weaving an elusive path underneath the belly of a dark society. Apparently, Charlie had seen the writing on the wall before she had, but he professed Protestantism.

Those nights spent playing flashlight tag in the suburbs as an adolescent came in handy. Most of the kids that played with her went on to become detectives and undercover agents. Moreover, they excelled at it. She had learned self-preservation from the best. The rules of a polite society faded with the arrival of an arid night, where common sense became as bright as day. In the dark, a person's actions spoke louder than appearances. Face value ruled.

The professors that she had recently encountered did not play games. Their authentic ardor raised every hair on the back of her neck as she closed the door of the apartment behind her. Donna met her taxi at a street a small distance away, so that her departure would not be obvious to those that inhabited the shared housing. Opening the passenger door, she slipped into the seat and took a deep breath. Donna felt confidant that she had eluded those who had been targeting her, even if it proved temporary.

Donna waved the taxi off at the airport and headed for a pay phone. Putting a few silver coins in the slot, she dialed. The familiar sound on the touch-tone phone soothed her.

"Hello," a husky male voice answered.

"Dad," she called in a hushed, unsure voice.

"Donna? What's up?" He asked, immediately sensing something amiss.

"I have been singled out for reasons that I don't understand. Students on campus say that Nicholas Hapsberg, an immortal financial sorcerer, is behind it. I'm grabbing the research job at Woodsport and catching a plane for the beach house now. I've gotta run. I'll write when I get there."

"Are you in trouble? Many corporations declare themselves immortal. Sounds very serpentine."

"Yes, I think I am in trouble. I ran into a group of academics, which don't appreciate answers or questions. Well, I think I stumbled onto something and gotta run."

"Alright," he interrupted her. "Go. Write me when you settle." Then he hung up with a click.

Donna sighed as she restored the receiver to the metal hook. Her father had been in the military. A former boyfriend admired his manner, which she had taken for granted until the young, proud, naval enlistee mentioned it. Her parents went into operational mode with the first whiff of something being askew, never trusting the circumstances. She could catch up with her parents later, just like her traveling companions.

Chapter Four

Rising above dark circumstances
Sheds light on the subject

Tune Reference: *Into the Night*
----Benny Mardones

AFTER SHE LANDED in the Boston airport, Donna sought a pay phone and dialed an unfamiliar number. She listened to the sequence of notes played as she pushed the touch-tone phone, the sound of her ticket to safety. Though not as intense as Charlie, another person in her life understood and had already garnered the support of a community.

"Hi," a young man answered at the other end of the line.

"Eric, hi, it's Donna. I've decided to come to Woodsport and do research.

"What!" Eric exclaimed, delighted with her news.

Donna heard him pause for a moment. She could hear his breathing accelerate. Glancing at the people racing through the Boston streets and driving fast cars that darted in and out of parking spaces, Donna bounced on one foot. She impatiently waited for Eric to finish his thoughts.

"Let me guess. You are at the airport and grabbing the quickest shuttle in a few minutes."

"Yep," she answered casually. "Let's go out for a beer later this evening. I am at the Boston airport and I don't want to be overheard."

Listening to the undercurrents of her request, he replied in the drawl of a rejected hound dog, "OK, you can tell me later. See ya at seven o'clock tonight at the Blue Heron tavern." Then he returned his focus to his own adventures. "I've got a lot to tell you. You would not believe what is happening here."

Donna smiled at his enthusiasm. Apparently, not the only one onto something, she rejoiced that she had kept up with this relationship. Despite her heavy workload, she kept Eric informed of her pursuits at the university. He always found life interesting, though maybe not quite as life-threatening. The ability to fold and run came important in science.

She hurried past the glass doors of the airport and climbed into the shuttle van. Then she took her second deep breath for the day. She felt another step further away from those who had been pursuing her at the university.

Donna could feel the air in the vehicle become balmy as the shuttle came closer to the cape. The driver dropped her off on a corner street under an antique street lamp. Donna walked hurriedly towards the small beach house a few blocks away. Stepping on the green slate leading to the blue, wooden porch steps, she saw the cottage from the eyes of the hunted seeking a refuge. This sudden change in perspective made her feel uneasy, as if somewhere along the way she had lost her innocence with the fading memories of childhood vacations. At least she had a base, she told herself, and she had someone to talk to tonight. She felt lucky. Not the bright green kind of luck, but the more serious tone of blue luck, like the trim on the screened door that squeaked when she pulled it ajar to place her key in the locked front door. Blue luck pertained to the fortune of making the most of one's resources without the distraction of needing more.

She opened the door and dropped her bags on the oval braided rug in the living room. They kept this house simple in order to keep the focus on fun and play. She checked out the two bedrooms and kitchen. Nothing seemed amiss, remaining as clean and inviting as her family last left it. Once she had made her inspection, Donna retrieved her suitcase and backpack from the living room. She deposited them in the plainly decorated room with a twin bed and a bunk, rather than seize the master bedroom.

Intending to conceal her arrival from anyone who casually wandered in the cottage, she quickly arranged her things between the closet and a few drawers as if they had been there for several months. Then she grabbed her keys and hurried out the backdoor. She found the sandy path at the edge of the vegetation surrounding the yard. Taking off her shoes, she walked on the grass bordering the path. Only a highly-skilled expert would be able to find her footprints mixed in with the sand and grass. Donna heard the familiar and distinct rhythm of the small waves rolling on the beach about a hundred yards away. She pressed on and climbed over the logs haphazardly lining the last half of the path, sensing that nobody would be able to trace her steps here.

She needed to think and make connections with the soothing melody of the waves. They always seemed to speak to her as the salty mist cleared her head, making room for her mind to play with her steps like a gymnastics routine. If she could relax with the rhythmic waves, solutions emerged as a dream from the tumbling froth. Donna waded up to her ankles in the gray-blue waters and watched the white foam swirl around her feet. Though relatively warm, the sudden winter coolness rose to her head like a splash. She cupped her hands and brought some of the salty waves directly on her face. Then she looked towards the misty horizon. Today, visibility remained blurry in the distance.

She dropped down on a thick log near her and momentarily focused on her breath. A breeze dried the water on her face. The sensation seemed reassuring rather than cold. Looking down at the tiny waves encroaching her position on the log, she felt minor amusement. A slight smile tugged at the upper corners of her lips. She couldn't help but feel relief, as she allowed the wind to take her lingering troubles away. Taking few minutes for reflection, Donna centered herself and deliberated her next move. In the branches of blossoming bush, she spied the rapid fluttering wings on a brown hummingbird. Fascinated by its fast grace, Donna imagined the bird communing with wood nymphs. The bird's color matched the branches and could easily be mistaken for a fat twig, if the vibration had not been so exuberant.

Armed with sense of joy in being welcomed in familiar territory, Donna resolved to check in with her new boss at the labs. The cool, smooth rhythms of the ocean waves comforted and reassured her. Comparing the sensation to her previous environment, a shudder ran up her spine as another thought disturbed her countenance. Besides wanting to be sure that she had the job, she wanted to see if he had been alerted by those responsible for her abrupt departure. One could never be sure where a spider's web ended. Rising from the log, she studied the movement of water as the hummingbird sped on to other flowers along the cape. Noting that the tide had come in, Donna quickly donned her shoes and journeyed back up the hill, taking care to disguise her steps. There were only a few people on the beach today and they were almost four hundred yards away, far enough to remain absorbed by their own worlds and disinterested in her activity.

Rather than return to the cottage, she opted for some stairs that led from the beach to the town on the bluff. She followed the walkway towards the labs about a mile away. Obtaining a map of the labs at the security gate, she brushed away remaining traces of sand from the beach and headed for the geophysics complex. She made herself appear as casual and fresh as a tourist.

Finding Dr. McClendon's office, Donna announced her arrival to the receptionist and waited. A few minutes earlier, a softly-grinning man with a mustache emerged from behind the closed door. He sized her up and beamed warmly. "Come in," he said, almost pulling her into the office before closing the door behind her.

"You must be the researcher for the resistivity modeling and seismic profiling," he surmised as he shook her hand for introductions. Donna nodded and answered, "Yes, I came a little early to settle in."

"Great, we can get started immediately, if that is alright with you," he offered, almost rubbing his hands together in glee.

Donna nodded and quickly glanced around the room. Nobody had told this man about her abrupt flight from the university. Perhaps she had hit the end of the spider's web that had threatened to enclose her. She noticed the votive next to the Kuan Yin statue on a table innocuously placed in a corner. Various pictures of Chinese masters graced the walls of the room, along with a few random displays of simple marital arts weapons. None of the weapons appeared particularly threatening, because their violence relied on the skill of the user rather than the weapon itself. This spiritual, nonaggressive man contrasted greatly with the volatile academics in Dallas.

Dr. McClendon showed her around the office and labs. She reviewed the data for one project and made suggestions. Then she completed paperwork for the administrators and agreed to start the following morning.

A few hours later, Donna walked to the entrance of the Blue Heron tavern and pushed the blue shutters of the door aside. She found Eric seated at a table towards the end of the dining room. A lighted hurricane lamp shone beside him, reflecting off his blonde hair and mustache, making them appear almost golden. He rose to hug Donna with wide, open arms and flashed her an even more golden smile. She felt immediate comfort by the embrace of her spirited friend.

They sat down across from each other. Donna eyed Eric's half-emptied pale golden beer and ordered a dark stout. She suspected that she had known him before in many lifetimes, never tiring of his wisdom. Donna sensed that he had been one of the first pilgrims or refugees on the planet Earth. She loved him for always being there, never needing to seek him. In college, he had sought her frequently, compelling her to make time for him. He became her friend, someone who needed her more than she realized. Never running away from danger, Donna understood that she faced a different challenge. Unlike the former environment, this place harbored her. With Eric, love had never been a question, however physical interaction would have provided an even greater distraction from the issues that fueled the attraction.

Eric looked at her earnestly. "I've only been here for six months but it has changed the entire way I view the world." Without further hesitation, he elapsed into a hurried discourse, "You must meet Dr. Stephen, the researcher in neurology. He is so cool. He gets everyone together for these squid hunts at night. He takes the neurons and we eat the squid. Squids have the largest neuron cells for research, ya know. Dr. Stephen's research is amazing---the things he is finding...the things all of us are learning. It is like quantum biology. If only the world only knew the things these scientists are doing in their closets. Now they must publish their results in obscure journals so they don't lose their funding. Did you know that you can build a radio transmitter out of red blood cells? Did you know that your brain waves could be transmitted via the Schumann-alpha waveguide that encircles the globe? That the DNA could transmit light like a laser? We are so much more than what the publishers let us print."

Donna slid back in her chair in a daze. Like a college professor, Eric savored his discourses. Heartened by his enjoyable presentation, she gained distance on her own problems after a trying day. His outlook seemed refreshing. Focusing on the soft flame in a hurricane lamp across the room, she saw its light reflected in the dark window overlooking the cape. The gradations of the glow penetrated the black waves that spread out into the distance. In the recess of her memory, she recalled the first ship, a platform with a bubble over it. She saw the bubble opening and the passengers stepping onto a large rock. One fell and skinned her knee, drawing the first blood on the earth. Eric's soul had been there in another form, and as usual he spoke from the depths of human experience.

Like a spy coming in from the cold, Eric pulled Donna in without ever questioning her abrupt arrival. He operated in the quantum world as well as studied it. In an instant, he took her understanding of her world and gave it a quantum leap. He had yet to ask her why she had fled the university. In his world where time went on, it didn't seem to matter. She felt her previous fear and worry vanish in his company.

"I know," she ventured as she continued to stare into the darkness enveloping the hurricane lamp. She wanted to bridge this new-found world into the events of the past week. She wanted to pin him down like charting a data point for perspective and position. As usual, his warm openness moved her to the point of reciprocation. They always worked this way; each complemented the other with their revelations in a rather competitive way. When it became her turn to top him, she waited for her words to settle into total shock on his face. Knowing that Eric had not anticipated her ready intrusion into his world, she dove into a place where he felt alone, no matter how many friends he cultivated.

Then she faced him, erupting on a lengthy rebuttal. "It is that way in many subjects from college english to history. I asked too many questions at the university and had to run. It was like I was questioning the Santa Claus myth. Ever wonder why college literature portrays only tragic figures such as Madame Bovary and losers such as those in *Light in August*?" Still watching his reaction, she quickly added, "Don't forget *The Wasteland* or *Brave New World*. Is it prophetic or are we already there? The educational system embeds tragedy into the American intellect. The scary thing is that the winners write the history texts. Why don't they just come out and say that the Americans also dumped opium during the Boston Tea Party? I feel like I am just coming off a bad trip. Suddenly, everything seems clearer. Over the past several weeks, I've learned that clarity threatens some people, which is scarier. I want to get beyond the illusions. Illusions are a very expensive risk, like academic smoke and mirrors."

Eric's eyes hinted at his understanding as Donna continued, "A distant relative once worked for Flying Tiger Airlines, the company which later became Federal Express. The airlines actually began during WWII in the Golden Triangle. I don't think the runs really closed after the Opium Wars; they just left the high seas for the high skies. This person left after figuring it out. A fellow graduate student worked with Ross Perot to help find MIAs in Viet Nam, but the drug trade and Pepsi stopped that quest. You know, Nixon was at a Pepsi convention in Dallas on the day of the JFK assassination...they once had real coke in the real thing. Now it is illegal, but you can go to either Chicago or Mexico for the stuff with the real pep. Maybe that's why these places seem always bankrupt."

Eric smiled slightly and tossed his head just enough to avoid calling attention to their table. He liked the way Donna always complemented him with a trump.

"We should all be in hiding," he answered slightly amused. "Sounds like the Knights of Malta all over again."

"The geology profession is laced with them. It lends new meaning to Pan Am Air, like it is another job description. They may have been the biggest donors to the university that I just fled. Years ago, they used their geology profits to start a new company in electronic instrumentation and calculators. These people go after popes, princesses, and presidents rather than flighty blondes and closet scientists," Donna commented. Looking around, she relaxed in the easygoing pub, "I feel relatively safe here."

Eric replied with his trump, "Few realize that Marilyn Monroe was a powerful anti-nuclear activist, who spoke her mind on Nixon as well as the Alger Hiss investigation. RFK later reopened the Hiss case as attorney general. The case proved bogus, and JFK put Ed Murrow in charge of the US Information Agency. Monroe lost one of her marriages to the anti-communist investigations. Remember, the husband who wrote *The Crucible*?"

"Monroe didn't run. Those who name themselves after presidents, don't pursue affairs with them. Innuendo makes for great marketing, especially if you are an actress," Donna quietly observed. Long before her birth, her perception of that time in US history had been framed by her family's personal experiences. She felt as if she had lived during that period, but possessed the emotional distance to see it as hindsight.

"Generally, artists are braver than scientists," Eric observed.

Donna gulped as another though crossed her mind. "JFK was already married with family before doing intelligence operations with Jackie. He ran for president as a WWII vet, and chose a non-threatening nazis operative as his partner in the White House. De Gaulle, the French president, sided with socialism and Jackie acted as a counter-weight to the Wall Street barons, who had funded both sides of the world wars. Did you know that the New York psychiatrist that supervised Monroe's doctor in California later served as Jackie's shrink after the assassination?"

A dark silence fell that seemingly shattered the glow of the small votive on the table between them. Donna gazed at it transfixed. Eric softly shook his head as he stared absently at her and the melting glow. He savored a few sips of his beer and waited for the effect on his senses. Experience had taught him to carefully weigh Donna's insights.

"People don't realize that both JFK and Jackie had been in intelligence operations. Jackie's stepfather had helped start the CIA---backgrounds like those just don't go away." Donna swallowed hard, remembering the effect of her own family's background on her life. "Jackie's mother dated Oswald's handler, a nazis double-agent called De Mohrenschildt, perhaps a triple agent, if you count his role in US geologic enterprises."

Eric shifted uncomfortably in his chair and looked over his shoulder. "Gotta know your geologists."

Not only had the attendants started to curiously eye the bright couple, a few late customers filled nearby tables. Tensing her shoulders, Donna seemed uneasy with the crowd. She did not hesitate when Eric offered, "Let's go."

With a light friendly wave to the waiters, Eric escorted Donna out of the pub. They walked down the block in the opposite direction from Donna's cottage. When they were away from any stray eavesdroppers, Eric teased, "How about coming down to the labs tomorrow after work? I think there are a few jobs for runaway geologists, especially those who accept plate tectonics. You can help us analyze the data from the volcanism at Mount Saint Helens. Pele speaks!"

Donna could almost feel his whimsical smirk as they turned the corner and headed towards the cottage. Eric invoked the Hawaiian god of volcanism, Pele, in his understanding of science. The geologists initially proposing plate tectonics had practically been burned at the stake in another 1950's inquisition, even though McCarthyism probably had nothing to do with it. Now the world accepted plate tectonics, as much as habitation on a globe. Compared to the recent events of her life and world perspective, the revolutions in geology seemed light. She smiled as they turned and began climbing the gradual hill towards her cottage. As they trudged upwards together, Donna related the events of the past month as best as she could, though they still bewildered her. She relied on Eric for understanding. He could reframe almost anything towards a logical conclusion.

Suddenly, he stopped and looked into the starlit sky above them. It seemed peaceful compared to the revelations in their discussion and he felt assured by the world above. A pair of roaming black dogs appeared in front of them. The labrador retrievers were out for a casual jaunt around the neighborhood, and they ignored Donna and Eric and continued down the street with scarcely a nod in their direction. Clearly, they did not want their owners to catch up with them.

Something about the sudden appearance of the black dogs shook Eric slightly. "Did you let Carrie know that you were not going to London? Have you heard from her?"

Donna turned and faced Eric. "No, if I had told her, then they might have bothered her. We planned to fly to Rome together." Then she sighed and glanced at the sky with a hint of anguish. "I ran," she emphasized as she looked at him directly. "Carrie possesses a second sense about these things, almost like a cat. We'll have to catch up later."

She hurriedly walked on towards the cottage and Eric silently joined her. He had not seen her for at least six months and nothing had changed about her, except that she seemed less mysterious and scarier. Her decision to drop everything and run jarred him. For the first time, he glimpsed into the world of spooks with cloak and daggers. He felt grateful for the reality check because it explained some of his own experiences, though the awakening still seemed rude.

She stopped again. Looking in the direction of the cottage, Donna nudged Eric and stepped back a few paces into the shadows. A van with flashing yellow lights was working on the telephone wires adjacent the house. Without offering any explanation to Eric, Donna boldly approached the workmen at the site. "They're keeping you guys busy tonight. Is there a problem?"

"Just putting in an extra line. Routine. Do you live around here?"

"Just down the street. I am looking for the owner of the black dogs that are running loose. There has been a rabies outbreak in the area," Donna said, improvising as she spoke. She knew how to spin a quick lifesaving-alibi so that even she believed it.

Instead of returning to the cottage, Donna continued walking down the block with a friendly wave to the crew and wishes for a quick job. Eric noticed her sudden deviation in plans and stayed beside her. A few yards away, she finally explained to him, "Let's wait until they are gone. I don't want to go back to the cottage now. What about showing me the geophysics buildings tonight?"

Eric gestured his bewilderment while simply agreeing, "Sounds like a good idea to me. Let's go. I feel comfortable with the security there."

Stepping out of the shadows, a clean-shaven man approached them from the opposite direction. He greeted them, "Hey have you seen two black dogs running around? They don't seem to want to go home."

"Well, you know how it is on a night like this...taking in the sites...with telephone crews prowling around. They are up there by the flashing yellow lights," Donna said.

"Thanks," the man smiled and hurried after his dogs.

Chapter Five

The old nymphs are heroes,
No matter how small or imperceptible

Tune Reference: *Hero*

----Enrique Iglesias

ERIC AND DONNA strolled back into the town and walked under the street lamps leading to the labs, located on the far end of the town. Near the edge of the cape, the growing heaviness in the salt air filled the atmosphere as water lapped on the nearby beach. Donna relaxed as they approached the buildings and waved at the security officer in the lighted booth at the entrance.

Showing Eric her new office, Donna ushered him inside one of the buildings and switched on a fluorescent light. Immediately the room became filled with a bright light that revealed an array of computer workstations. Colorful geologic maps and shelves of rocks graced the walls of the office.

"Dr. McClendon needs some resistivity modeling for the hazardous waste sites," Donna remarked as she led Eric around. Though already familiar with the office from past work with Dr. McClendon, he toured the room and listened to her interpretations. A map on the table caught his attention. Eric lingered over the map, shooting Donna a puzzled glance after he looked up.

"I am also doing some seismic profiling for the San Francisco region," Donna explained. "An architect from MIT is designing earthquake-proof buildings. These are the machines they use. It's relatively straightforward."

Donna slowly walked around the room while Eric studied the map. Finally deciding to move on, she quietly nodded at Eric. Though the map absorbed his thoughts, he dropped his focus as if politely waiting for her cue. Such encounters often transcended time and they touched other worlds during their investigations. Tonight he dwelt in her world. Eric waited for Donna for an ending, like a period or another mark of punctuation. Like other scientists they often communicated without words, using maps, numbers, and graphs. In personal interactions, they preferred gestures indicating complete concepts and full-bodied ideas. Words existed merely as a formality, serving to ground the interaction in the mundane. After she realized that she had captured his attention, Donna verbalized, "Where's your building?"

"The paleontologists work two doors down by the biology offices. Let's go there. We'll find a better view of the water," Eric said with a smile.

He led her to his area and explained some of the projects. When they had finished their survey, they stopped for a moment to gaze at the black waters of the cape. The salt from the ocean lightly hung in the air. They remained silent for several seconds while each reflected on the sudden turn of events that had brought them together again.

Glancing at her wristwatch, a sudden chill ran up Donna's back. "It's already half-past seven. Checking on the phone company can wait. I need a hot shower."

Eric noticed her panicked stare at the ground beneath her feet. Mournfully looking at the pavement, a thought crossed his mind. He straightened his back and puffed his chest a little, "Say, I have some friends who have use of the Frank Lloyd Wright house on the spit---it once was a school for architects. One of them works with the lab computers for the university. They invited me over for a glass of wine later this evening. You'd like them. Want to join me?"

Donna nodded with a light shrug and followed her friend. They quickly turned off the lights and locked the door behind them. An ebony sky had settled over the cape while they had been inside. Donna tried to adjust her eyes to the night, but visibility remained poor. She wondered how sailboats found their way across the waters. Something about the darkness seemed to unsettle her and she arched her back.

Trusting her instincts as they walked over the wooden planks on a dimly lit boardwalk, Donna slowly floated a new idea, "Do they have resident housing for scientists who have temporary positions with the labs?"

Eric eyed her curiously, but a drop in his shoulders indicated his relief as he slowly answered, "Yes, there is, but we will have to ask around. Perhaps Dr. Lorenzo knows. He is the one who we meet tonight." Then he added, "Looking for a place to stay?"

"Uh yeah," Donna replied. Shaking her head in resolution, she studied the patterns in the ground of wood. Even in the darkness, a few distinct markings became apparent under the moonlight and artificial glow of a streetlamp.

They walked off the boardwalk and headed down a gravel road leading to the spit. The house loomed in the distance like a lighted ship. Eric and Donna trudged up a hill and found a door at the back of the house. Facing the cape, two entry doors could be seen on either side and in the back. In contrast to the style of southern mansions, the house missed a main entrance. As if to sidestep the grandeur of false fronts, Donna watch Eric choose the door used by the service people near the back of the kitchen. A quaint, wooden, screen door masked the blue door leading into the pantry. The color lent her a vague sense of familiarity, being the same color as the cottage and swinging doors of the Blue Heron.

Eric rapped on the blue door graced by an incandescent porch lamp. Within seconds a towering, gracious gentleman emerged from behind the door.

"Eric, how wonderful to see you," the olive-skin man greeted, as he ushered them out of the night and into the soft glow inside the house. He smiled at his youthful guests as they entered his abode.

"I brought a friend," Eric told him as he pulled Donna near him. "She just arrived from the Midwest this afternoon. This is Donna. She'll be joining Dr. McClendon's geology group in the lab."

A woman appeared from the kitchen and extended a feminine handshake with a shy grin. "Nice to meet you," she said.

"Margarette," Dr. Lorenzo announced. "Eric brought another scientist for the lab. A geologist from...where did you say?" he pondered audibly, like weighing a small valuable coin between his fingers.

"Texas," Donna admitted in the warm presence of the couple who had won her trust.

"Oh, Texas," the soft-spoken Italian man murmured as he ushered them into a sitting room beyond the kitchen doors. Waist high glass windows encased the sitting room on all three sides, offering almost a panoramic view of the cape. He told them that the room had once been a screened porch, a way to connect the habitants with the world outside.

"Can I pour you a glass of wine?" the Italian host offered, while Margarette brought out crackers and tapenade.

She placed the tray next to some slices of grapes, apples and oranges on the table. "Please, sit down," she requested in English with the hint of a Swiss accent.

Donna chose a glass of Merlot before opting for a chair next to Eric's at the round table. A few candles strategically placed in the room provided plenty of light. Dr. Lorenzo and Eric quickly embarked on talk about the latest project they shared in the labs while Margarette interjected comments. Not only did Margarette play cheerleader for the lab projects, but she also seemed to be the philosopher. The commotion allowed Donna a few moments to absentmindedly gaze out the windows overlooking the cape. The effects of the red wine began to soothe the tremors of her day.

"Do you have a place to stay?" the man asked as he glanced at Donna. He had deftly brought up the question as if on cue.

"She's looking for one," Eric chimed. His quick response took control of the conversation before Donna could steer it in another direction.

The man whirled around to face Eric. Fathoming the deep friendship between the newcomer and Eric, he returned his attention to Donna. Margarette grinned brightly at the woman and nodded.

"Dr. Avery's studio is available," Dr. Lorenzo softly offered. He knew the particular comings and goings of various professors intimately. Resident housing on the cape became a commodity amongst the international scientists.

Donna relaxed even more under the effects of the red wine, pleased at his admission. For the meanwhile she felt safe and could enjoy the social occasion. The charming scene contrasted greatly with the chaotic campus that she had fled.

"How wonderful!" Margarette exclaimed, clasping her hands exuberantly together. "Avery will be so happy to hear that his studio is already rented." Immune from the hierarchy of academics, Margarette reveled in a first-name relationship with all the scientists.

The evening passed as smoothly as the sailboats across the cape. During the course of discussion, Donna stared into the grey sky outside and contemplated the effects of her recent journey. Margarette noticed her absence from the conversation and approached her directly. "Come, please help me with the next course. I have some red and yellow bell peppers to prepare. Do you and Eric like bell peppers?"

Eric and Donna quietly smiled and nodded. Although, Margarette was Swiss; she ran a dinner like an Italian where multiple courses became punctuated by periods of wine and philosophical conversation. Donna followed Margarette through the nightly shadows enveloping the house into the brightly-lit kitchen. She helped chop a few yellow, red, and green peppers for Margarette and watched quietly as the lightly-freckled Swiss woman stir-fried the colorful combination in an earthy, stainless steel skillet. She wondered about the extent of Margarette's understanding of the research at the labs on a spiritual level. Margarette stopped Donna as she carried the tray of bell peppers down the corridor of picture windows overlooking the spit. "It's a special moment," she observed, gazing outside the picture window overlooking the dimly lighted cape.

Donna carefully watched Margarette thoughtfully look at the distant horizon. With relief, Donna sighed and eyed the starlit sky outside the window. A single thread ran through the chaotic events of the day. Though too premature to determine this thread's significance, she recalled fleeing the university to avoid being targeted. Now she enjoyed an intimate dinner across the country with new friends.

Donna nodded at the woman. She felt that she knew her from somewhere before. Without saying a further word, the two women walked down the hallway to the candlelit-dining room. Eric beamed at the women as they deposited the trays of food on the wooden table. Dr. Lorenzo smiled and thanked them. He deftly poured more wine as the women joined the men at the table. Dr. Lorenzo seemed to be the only one in the room who heard her. He eyed her with calm, brown eyes and a slightly curious smile.

Out of the ensuing silence, Margarette offered a warm interjection, "We see these things from other countries." Both Dr. Lorenzo and Donna turned their attention towards Margarette, who seemed all too quick to jump on this topic. "The research that comes from the labs is so radically different from that which is provided in the media and texts. If the results don't fit what they think the world wants to hear, then they ignore it. Then they don't fund it. Without funding the scientists have no way to support themselves."

"It is very competitive at the universities," Dr. Lorenzo softly added. "Though, I think people want to know. There must be an easier way to explain some of these ground-breaking, high-level ideas to others. The gap between what scientists know and the general public is widening.

"And a lot of static in-between," Eric quoted Donna. He had also heard Donna earlier. In this small group where knowledge became a dedicated pursuit, this revisited revelation created a slight shudder in the air. Quietly they all watched the vibration come and go as it dissipated out of the glass windows and across the cape's dark waters. The perspective relaxed them. Donna welcomed the European perspective. For centuries, ideas and innovations had been birthed on their soil, while life seemed to hang on to one dinner celebration after another. Would the Renaissance been as successful in the U.S. as in Europe? Would it been ignored if it never made it into the media? Despite the wars, some sense of the divine had survived, even if the conquerors looted the museums. Though the populace never completely understood, they still coveted art.

Donna sighed, expressing relief that simple geologists could stay out of the fray. She avoided those who never understood what they wanted, whether they sought to own or possess. She peddled dirt, the dirt of ages. The same dirt that existed under the feet of both artisans and their public. Geologists served as the scientists who studied this dirt through time. They knew which mountains existed at the time of Rome and what the continents looked like during the age of the dinosaurs. The terrain served as the background music for the living that continued. Few realized the subtle influences.

"Dr. Lorenzo, it has been a pleasure as usual," Eric interrupted after a brief moment of silence as each member of the group reflected on the darkness outside the room. The exchange of knowledge amongst friends left everyone feeling secure and reassured. He stood and offered his hand to the professor. They both stood and pulled Donna closer to them.

"Would you like to stay in Avery's apartment for this evening?" Dr. Lorenzo inquired as he waved at Margarette. Hurriedly, he added, "Margarette, do you have the key?"

"Oh yes, it's right over here," Margarette answered as she reached inside a desk in an adjacent room. She quickly handed the key to Eric as she instructed him, "Please show the apartment to Donna. We are tired for the evening and must get up early for a trip to Boston in the morning. We'll be back after the weekend and we can settle the arrangements then."

Margarette ushered them quickly towards the hallway leading to the kitchen door. Donna and Eric politely waved, offering few words except thanks and hurried into the night. They walked down the hill and towards the studio apartments near the university labs.

"I think I know where it is," Eric said as he pointed Donna towards a building and up some stairs. "It is at the far end. You'll have a private deck." When they reached the top, Eric placed the key in the door and it opened. For a moment they were greeted by darkness, and then Eric turned on the lights, illuminating a simple studio apartment with a kitchenette. A modern glass shower adjoined the bedroom off to the side. "I think you'll like it here," he added.

"Yes, it is great. I'll get my things tomorrow. This evening has been so calming that I almost forgot that I am on the run. It's such a contrast," Donna answered. Softly, she observed, "...like two polarities with a lot of static in between."

Pausing briefly in silence, her eyes met Eric's wry resignation. He looked at her uncomfortably, realizing that there was more to be said about her circumstances. Meeting his stare, Donna shrugged slightly with a particular lightness.

"...But I'm moving," she reflected. "And I am moving in," she announced happily with a touch of chagrin.

"Good for you. Pele would be proud," Eric responded as he put his arm around her and hugged her gently. "I'll be back after work tomorrow afternoon."

"Thanks," Donna responded with light exuberance. "It has been wonderful. I really enjoyed meeting Dr. Lorenzo and Margarette. I couldn't ask for a nicer time or anything else." After moment of reflection, she rejoined, "Except maybe a toothbrush." She followed Eric out the door. "I'll walk with you some of the way. I saw an open drugstore around the corner."

A few minutes later, Donna returned to the apartment with a small bag of groceries and examined the room more closely. She felt at home. Nothing about the room caused her to feel alarm. She washed and settled in the bed, finally retiring for the evening and tucked away from the world's chaos.

Chapter Six

True love

Finds us like a

Feather in the wind

With the subtleties

Tune Reference: *All My Love*

----Led Zeppelin

DONNA MET DR. McClendon at his office early the next morning. He handed her the front page of a newspaper as he lit a votive candle near a statue of the goddess of compassion. Donna glanced at the headlines and hid a gasp. Dr. McClendon glanced at her, as he saluted the statue, which represented the divine feminine archetype of compassion rather than sexless procreation. The headlines mentioned a train wreck in Italy that had resulted in almost a hundred deaths. The wreck had occurred close to the university where she once intended to study.

She sat down on a chair near the computer workstation. Raising her head and staring at the blank wall in front of her, Donna wondered whether any of her friends were on that train. Her head swam with the events of the past few days. Donna's thoughts connected the event to those questioning her at the university. They peddled the academic commodity of fear, the calling card of the *nadas*.

"A terrorist group claims responsibility for the train-bombing," Dr. McClendon explained.

Putting the paper aside, Donna focused on her work. Dr. McClendon stared at her. Unable to dismiss his intensity, Donna turned her head to the side and hid her anguish from his gaze. Facing the shelves of research papers filled against the far wall, she leaned back in her chair with a sigh. She thought about *whom could she trust and what could she trust?* The events leading to her sudden change of plans seemed surreal in comparison to the black and white reality portrayed in the headlines.

"Come join me for martial arts at the Exercise Club. I'm teaching a new class tonight," Dr. McClendon told her.

Having made his agenda clear, he quietly waited for Donna's reply. He had served as an officer with the marines during the Viet Nam war, and had skillfully managed to survive through intention and insight. Within seconds, Donna gave him her full attention. Contemplating his abrupt change of the topic, she could see the answer as much as she saw the problem. An eerie sense that he understood her predicament crossed her mind. He seemed very intuitive in a cultivated sort of way. If she truly became a fugitive, then a little bit of training and insight from those with a record of success might come in handy. She faithfully clung to her convictions. Dire circumstances could be challenged by looking for the thread of fortune, which led the way out of a complex labyrinth. Whether through courage or skill, she had never failed to find that lucky thread.

"When is it?" Donna asked.

"Seven o'clock Thursday evening at the Woodsport Exercise Club," he told her with a beaming grin and smooth bow. He seemed happy to have her join him.

Donna's surfacing fears lifted with his invitation. The whole room suddenly seemed lighter and brighter. Together she and Dr. McClendon steered the conversation towards the purpose of their meeting. He booted a program on the computer and began to explain, "An architect from MIT needs this seismic data to build the next high rises in Oakland, California. We have the seismic data for the San Francisco area from the past five years. First, we need to convert the raw data into a seismic profile, and then use these models to predict the next earthquake tremor."

"Like transforming a geologic event into the wavelength or frequency?" Donna questioned. Her work could have major positive impact on the lives of millions of people, if she did her work carefully.

"Yes, the engineers use the information in placing the internal support system of the building. It's like high school physics. If the distance between the support pillars matches the frequency of the earthquake, then the building will not shatter with the resonance. The building will move with the oscillations of the quake. Otherwise, the earthquake will hit the structure like an opera singer singing at a frequency to shatter glass."

Donna set back in her chair and sighed with relief. The prospect of preventing widespread destruction contrasted sharply with the newspaper headlines. She always enjoyed working on projects that offered a practical non-threatening application of science. Fascinated by the notion of resonance, Donna had viewed videos of the effects of high winds causing bridges to furl in the wind like they were metallic tidal waves. The collapse of the Tacoma Narrows Bridge around the 1940's had been filmed and still remained unbelievable. Metal had been reduced to a leather horsewhip snapping in the wind. During the First World War, soldiers sang as they marched to avoid generating a frequency with their steps that would collapse the bridge underneath their feet. She wondered what the Roman soldiers had done. According to an engineer from MIT, all the bridges standing today were based on the calculations of the ancient Romans. Ironically, their pursuit of world dominance granted them the peace-evoking title of having been the first bridge-builders. Not only did all roads lead to Rome, most bridges came from Roman engineers. Although scientists strongly suspected that they used too much cement in building bridges, nobody dared to deviate from the ancient Roman equations. Subsequent civilizations had not bothered to experiment with their own mortar and mix, probably due to time and money, which served as testament to the human drive to make connections.

Her mind centered on the newspaper headlines again. *What kind of Italians would blow their own bridges or transit system?* The train disaster appeared as an obnoxious abnormality given the fact that the world still trusted ancient Rome to build their bridges.

Dr. McClendon left, and Donna began to load the familiar seismic-profiling program. The task proved an interesting and sometimes tedious job, one that would allow time to meditate on these tangential questions. Minutes turned into hours. By the time Donna glanced at the clock, it read two o'clock, past the usual lunchtime. One of the benefits about being a researcher in a group of devoted scientists was the elimination of a schedule; her colleagues as well as herself followed their creative rhythms. She knew her own rhythm enough to know that she had better take a break and get something to eat before she exhausted herself, because the comeback would take longer like exponential decay.

She quietly stepped out of the computer lab without meeting anyone. She noticed that Dr. McClendon had apparently left for the afternoon. His desk in the nearby office appeared too organized for a temporary absence.

The scientific community had its strange laws of communication where it was acceptable to disappear on a research initiative, without saying a word. One never knew if the creative trail would hit pay dirt, so one never bothered to mention the wild goose chases that it took to get there, at least while in pursuit. It could be embarrassing if expectations were not met or if the results loomed too astonishing for the given theory. There existed many reasons why scientists lived in their closets or hid there to talk to the Divine.

Donna realized that she harbored no exception to this rule, and so she turned for the library after getting a falafel sandwich from a street deli. She hurried to the newspaper section for more information on the train wreck in Italy and glanced at the headlines. Skimming the article to determine whether any of her former classmates had been among the victims, Donna wondered if a group would claim responsibility for the terrorism. The article claimed that the bombing had been done in retaliation for the recent exposure of a secret government within Italy. Donna read further, shaking her head at how blind that she had been to Italian political affairs concerning her travel plans. Investigators had connected the secret Vatican financiers with the JFK assassination. Having the information that she needed to unravel the mysterious circumstances compelling her abrupt departure from Dallas, she neatly placed the newspaper back on the rack. Then she hurriedly left the library. The walk back to office lifted some of her shock. Returning to the office, she found Dr. McClendon seated at his desk.

"How's the seismic modeling going?" he asked. Being in a reflective mood, his soft stare into the distance calmed Donna. He smiled at her, pleased that somebody finally put all this data to practical humanitarian use.

"It's pretty straightforward," Donna said with a nod. She sighed quietly and dropped the tension in her shoulders. Swirling around in her desk chair, she expressed relief that he was the sort who would not pry into her world, being content with his own.

"Party on," he said waving her in the direction of the computer. Later, he peered into the room wearing a black cowboy hat on his head. "See ya tomorrow," he told her as he handed her a key to the office. Without a word, the gesture implied the responsibility in locking the doors behind her. He cut an imposing figure with his tall, compact frame and black hat. His light manner contrasted his attire, lending his blackness an air of mystery rather than opposition.

Donna shyly nodded at him before he smoothly stepped out of the room and out the door. He wore his costume from the southwest with ease. She knew that he had studied in Oklahoma. For someone authentically from the southwest, it wasn't a costume. Only the movies distinguished the bad guys from the good guys with colored hats. In the southwest, the color black served as an understated party announcement. Donna appreciated the thought of working for an individual, someone with enough character to be authentic. Reality kept the job interesting and served as an artistic balance to the dry logic of the science.

After locking up the office in the early evening, Donna headed for a pay phone before returning to her apartment. "Mom!" she called. "What's up?"

"Well, Uncle Ted landed in the hospital with broken ribs last night. It had been a surprise attack. This is the third time this month. His wife wants him out of government intelligence operations. Routine missions going haywire and he isn't that high up in the agency…"

Donna listened to her mother ramble.

"...And we can't seem to leave the house without finding bugs in our phone. Your father pulled several out last night after we came back from dinner. He seemed a little on edge...watching the entrance to the restaurant...don't know how those spies are getting into the house."

Donna tossed her head back and forth. Like the waves rolling across the cape, something always brewed. She had grown up with these occurrences. Dull roars from her family comforted her.

"And how's Aunt Janet?" Donna interrupted when her mother stopped to ponder the situation for a moment.

"Oh, she found her house bugged too. We think that it is because she is confronting the Texas Railroad Commission for putting too much chlorine in their drinking water out in West Texas. Ann Richards, the governor, called and wants to talk to her. They are finding that it involves a big chain of department stores in Dallas. It'll be the last time I shop there."

"Yeah, I know. Oswald's handler, Zapruder, and friends all worked for the same Dallas department store. Try changing that frame around. Why would a geologist be working in a department store to handle an alleged assassin, one who lives with associates of the CIA agent that JFK fired?... and associates that rented to JFK's father on the cape?" Donna questioned, before embarking on another story line. "The fired agent, former head of CIA, also worked with Jackie. He supposedly had Jung for a private counselor during WWII. Zapruder missed filming a famous news reporter underneath the Triple Overpass. Instead the young reporter got the scoop, not the the camera guy." Then she abruptly changed the topic and inquired, "How's Rachel?"

Her mother sighed. "It all goes back to the terrain...Your sister uncovered a crime ring, which stole gold from cadavers in San Antonio. A popular magazine wants to talk to her about it, but her supervisor on the police force is jealous. So she is lying low in the detective unit now."

"And Aunt Sue?" Donna asked, moving on quickly to make sure she covered most of her relations.

"Oh, she's being sued for trying to start up the Democratic Party after the last election. There isn't much left after the Republicans wiped out the local area."

None of this news stunned Donna, being familiar with the political patterns of the state.

"How are you doing?" her mother finally questioned her.

"Oh, I'm doing alright," Donna responded. "I'm a little upset over the train bombing in Italy. The transit went right by the university where I intended to pursue graduate studies. None of my friends were hurt, according to the newspaper. This time they targeted Italians rather than tourists. Some group associated with the Grey Wolves claims responsibility. I don't think that they publicly connected that Turkish terrorist group to NATO yet. They brought in a nazis to head the pentagon, after World War II. Remember, the same double-agent that betrayed US forces during the Battle of the Bulge?"

Pausing to reflect on the soldiers who had escaped the genocidal setup concerning one of the final battles with nazis in World War II, Donna's countenance brightened with the recognition of hope. A Commander Wolff had headed the Nazis SS in Italy and surrendered secretly to Allen Dulles, the man that JFK eventually fired after Bay of Pigs. Like Jackie, Dulles's nazis leanings had not been a threat to the presidency. However, Dulles's connection with the American businesses that profited during the Vict Nam war became the threat to the United States. The Bell Helicopter company, which employed Oswald's landowner, gained significantly with the Viet Nam war. With Dulles's brother as Secretary of State, Eisenhower warned about the military-industrial complex before he passed the presidency to another veteran of a world war. As the Italian government overturned the remaining fascist-nazis tentacles on free speech and independent thought, those refusing to fit the mold cast by the military-industrial complex became targets, a practice perfected after two world wars. As in Nazis Germany, one didn't have to be a pope, actor, or president to face persecution. The test for students at the university near the heart of the military-industrial complex had been to repeat the theologic ideology of C. S. Lewis, the nazis Oxford scholar who died on the same day as JFK. After taking this course and dodging the inevitable persecution, Donna deduced the threat of an old Wolff network on the pope with greater social skills than Virginia Wolff's tormentor, C. S. Lewis. Those who refused the doom of *Brave New World,* a form of revelations penned by another who died on the same day as JFK, also became targets. Pleased to zero in on essential issues with a relation, Donna eschewed the opportunity to make conjectures that only she and a few others could understand. She dove into the conversation to track the latest threads. Survival and the ability to thrive depended on connecting the dots. Pertinent threads could be teased out of the chaos for prosperity and life-sustaining measures.

"The geophysics work is amazing," Donna continued. "Saw Eric...and there is something going on at the cottage so a friend-of-a-friend got me into a studio apartment. It's great and I'm meeting lots of nice people. Tonight I'm learning martial arts at the local exercise club. The boss is teaching a class and I thought I'd better follow up. Looks like I could use the training," she added ruefully.

"OK, that sounds good," her mother encouraged.

"Oh, one other thing, Eric says that the Camelot myth actually had a reality," Donna said, changing the subject. "A linguist by the name of Goodrich places the legend in Camelon. Did you know that the Roman capital in Britain was called Camulodunon? Eric just returned from an expedition near Camelon."

"Like Santa Claus, there's a kernel of truth in most myths," she replied. "Take it easy. Love you."

Her mom hung up as Donna echoed her words 'love you,' then 'bye.' She placed the receiver on the hook and left the telephone booth.

Donna almost skipped back to her apartment. She loved talking to her relations. The beautiful waterfront view on a sunny day reassured her that she had come to the right place at this point in life. She felt like a feather in the winds steadily blowing across the cape, causing her to land lightly at her door two-flights-of-stairs high.

Chapter Seven

Sometimes freedom is found

In a simple touch,

Reminiscent of a devoted love

Tune Reference: *Separate Ways*

— —Journey

DONNA SLIPPED INTO the makeshift training hall and found Dr. McClendon surrounded by a motley crew of young men. He stood at least six inches above the smallest male in the group. Together they started stretching, assuming different poses depending upon body type and muscular tensions. Some students stretched on the floor; some braced against the wall, while others interacted with various bags and rubber bands hanging from the ceiling. Though accustomed to being the only female in a masculine setting, Donna relaxed when Dr. McClendon greeted her with a warm smile. Instead of staying close to the exit, she merged with the rest in the room.

"Find the way that is not forced," he reminded the group with a bellow.

Donna stretched her legs out on the soft wooden floor. Agreeing with his philosophy, she didn't push her muscles. Like the horse she had given the sociology professor, she chose to ride through recent events and avoid exploding trains or brainwashing psychologists brainwashing on the trail. The other members of the class quietly resumed their stretching. Later in the evening, she learned an exercise called "Circling Palms" that not only served as a block against attackers, but balanced acupuncture meridians. As a result she felt more at peace with the world than what she had experienced during the past two weeks. In the evening she walked back to the apartment and quickly fell into a deep restful sleep.

The next day she walked by the family cottage and saw that it was just as still and quiet as any other small vacation home. There were no signs of any other visitors since the evening with the work crew. Arriving at the office thirty minutes later, she found Dr. McClendon pouring over various geologic maps strewn across his desk.

"Enjoy the class?" he asked her as she busied herself with her next set of seismic data.

"Oh yeah, it's very relaxing. I loved the mediation set; it seems more balanced than other sets I've known," Donna replied as she made a mental note to somehow catch up with Eric this afternoon. The exercise belonged to another world, a Celtic domain of green dragons and merpeople. She could never take any martial-art discipline seriously, after having spent years playing touch football and night time flashlight tag with a multitude of cousins who never played by the rules. In fact, one could always count on the fact that they wouldn't. They could cut through any formality faster than anyone she knew and get straight to the point.

At lunchtime Eric arrived at the office and sought Donna. He waved a greeting to Dr. McClendon and joined Donna at her desk. "Dr. Lorenzo and Margarette invited you to dinner tomorrow afternoon. They have been asking about you," he said with a grin.

"Wait a minute," Dr. McClendon interrupted. "There's a lawyer who needs some help with a company just west of Boston. He's coming this afternoon. The meeting tonight will probably run into dinner," he speculated. "You could be asked to go into the field tomorrow afternoon to collect some data. He says it's an emergency."

Donna leaned back in her chair. She had scarcely been on the cape for a week before events started moving rapidly. Like a sailor noticing the sudden shift in wind velocity, Donna pondered the quickening of events. She charted her life, having found a distinct path. Even forks in the road had a weighted answer. In the end only one path suited her best. Donna decided to stick to her main purpose for being on the cape. "Tell Lorenzo and Margarette that I'd love a rain check. Science beckons."

Eric laughed, remembering all the late nights Dr. Lorenzo spent in the lab during Margarette's absence. Margarette enjoyed visiting her adult children in Europe and she often stayed several weeks with their families. This gave Dr. Lorenzo the opportunity to focus on his research while Margarette travelled.

Though unsure whether he wanted to dwell in an atmosphere of passions and risks, Eric left as quickly as he had entered. He sensed the intensity of Donna's thoughts, related to a world that he never fully understood. For her own part, Donna appeared reluctant to tell him about her perspective. As Eric fled the scene, Donna watched him leave. *How could she ever begin to explain a life that seemed so familiar to her and yet so alien to someone who had never needed to learn how to hide?* It reminded her of children who continued to play hide-and-go-seek, eventually making the pursuit a profession. *Had Eric ever learned to seek?*

After work, Donna followed the beach from the edge of town to her favorite log on the beach path from her family home. She sat down on the log and removed her sneakers. Rubbing her toes in the sand, she reflected on the plate that life and events had recently served her. She practiced the exercise set on her own and kept up with her training. Though, she had not finished unpacking her bags in the studio apartment, she could throw some clothes and toiletries together on a moment's notice. Her work on the seismic data came along well, so she could easily step away for a week or two and still make their deadline.

Despite the chaos in her present life, she always remained organized and efficient. Donna rose and stood on the log as she looked out to sea. Then she challenged herself by practicing her balance on the log as she walked back and forth across it. The routine resembled a feat from childhood that she never outgrew, like finger exercises before playing piano. Pacing on the log kept her thoughts light as she posed her questions from the past month and juggled them like small weighted balls. She needed to remain flexible in her thoughts, as her life changed quickly now.

The next day, Dr. McClendon and a blonde, middle-aged man of medium stature greeted her in the lab. "This is Eli Simpson, the gentleman I mentioned yesterday. We stayed awake until midnight discussing the project. He has hired the geology lab for consulting purposes."

Dr. McClendon turned towards the gentleman next to him with a wry, cautious grin. The gentleman, casually but neatly dressed in a striped polo shirt and blue jeans, stared at the floor a few moments before addressing Donna directly. Raising his brow, he subtly expressed surprise at finding an attractive consultant. "I need for you to collect some geophysical data on a site that we think is contaminated," Eli began. "We need to keep it quiet until I finish the investigation."

Donna looked at him, while gauging the seriousness of the request. Turning her head from side to side, she appeared amused by those in attendance, which included a casually dressed lawyer and a martial arts instructor, who sidelined as a scientific researcher. Carefully holding back his words with a hard swallow, Eli acknowledged Donna as a geologist who practically arrived only yesterday.

Donna turned away in her chair, shocked by the realization. She glanced at Dr. McClendon, who had chased Eric away like a patriarch with a shotgun. Despite her late arrival in the group, the two men stared deeply at her. The heaviness in their eyes bolted Donna to her position before them. Every professional knew that there were undercurrents to most worthwhile projects in today's world. Having already earned a reputation, Donna sensed that the recognition didn't only pertain to her expertise in geophysics; the imploring look in their demeanor pertained to intrigue, the very thing that she minimized in her life. Somehow Dr. McClendon must have picked up on this. Instead of looking the other way, he wanted to promote her savvy ability to swim through the undercurrents. Evidently, this talent appealed to Eli as well.

Rather than go quietly, Donna decided to play a card as a way of establishing boundaries. Lightly, but firmly shaking her head, she studied the papers on her desk and conveyed her refusal to do someone else's detective work, preferring to keep her geophysics job safe. Then she faced them both and boldly hung her head slightly with a slight sigh. With a roll of her eyes, she sent the nonverbal message that she had her own, unwanted dangers in life. Leveling her gaze at the lawyer in front of her, Donna cocked her head and fired a dead-eyed look to let him know that she did not want to purposely endanger her life.

Dr. McClendon leaned back with a thoughtful smile to consider the risks of Eli's project. With a wry grin, he acknowledged Donna's spunk, while admitting that he had not realized the degree to which she had been tempered like a sword in a hot fire. His reflections sobered him a bit and he waited for Eli's response. Folding his fingers together in a light clasp, he sensed that this young woman had seized a leadership position in a full swoop, while restraining the hormone-charged blindness that lead to unhealthy risk taking. Glancing at her out of the corner of his eye, he imagined that she held this position, despite being out-sized and out-maneuvered. He leaned back in his chair and softly tapped his fingers tips against each other. In this mild, meditative state, he savored the yin-yang balance of war and peace that he had experienced following his Viet Nam tour.

Eli gulped at Donna's challenge. Wishing to win her over, he answered with a hint of honesty in his voice. "The local city has recently found a new source of contamination in its drinking water. It isn't the local paper mill residue. We have traced the source to a factory that we suspect of using illegal hazardous substances to make their product." He paused briefly, before continuing, "We think that the employees are being hypnotized into making the products. They have no recollection of using these hazardous substances even though we are finding these contaminants in the product."

Donna remained silent during his response. Raising one brow in suspicion, she made Eli acutely aware of the line between fact and professional opinion. Eli's eyes searched Dr. McClendon before offering his final argument. He confided, "One of the employees lapsed into a hypnotic state and revealed an international conspiracy."

Donna sized up his observation before admitting, "You don't usually find international conspiracies for a little groundwater contamination." She recalled dozens of groundwater contamination sites that didn't involve conspiracy. Sometimes it was the local laundromat responsible for the contamination, sometimes the local gasoline station, and sometimes it was creosote from railroad ties made during the 1800's. None of these cases were ever the result of conspiracy; they simply pertained to an absence of foresight and human error.

Eli never answered her. Neither did Dr. McClendon. Appreciating their silence, Donna remained seated and fathomed the gravity of the situation. The silence also gave her the chance to pursue her own conclusions. Her thoughts flashed to the recent train bombing in Italy, though she could not presently make a logical connection. Many more questions, possibilities, and connections raced through her mind. Her thoughts ended with an image of Carrie traveling to Italy and she felt a slight chill, which she quickly shook off once she recognized it. She hoped that Carrie remained safe. Her thoughts returned to their offer, which she accepted. Dr. McClendon grinned and Eli thanked her.

Later in the week, Donna met the rest of the survey crew at the parking lot near the guard gate. A stocky brown-haired man in his mid-twenties lumbered out of one of the blue trucks. He carried a clipboard in his hand and rolled his eyes with a hint of annoyance as he showed her where she could stow her gear in the bed of the truck. He called to other members of the crew, who were slowly sipping coffee and staring dumbly out the front windshield.

Donna briefly waved at the men in the cab as she hurriedly placed her bags in the back. She did not want to be the one to wake them from their morning haze. The man with the clipboard left her to give last minute directions to the men in the other vehicle. Donna took a deep breath and swiftly inspected the contents of the truck, before she took time to arrange her gear. She noticed some gasoline spilling from one of the generators.

Whoever had placed the equipment in the vehicle had been careless or malicious. From the coldness of their reception, she suspected the later.

"Here's a map to the site," the man with the clipboard announced after she joined him at the front of the truck. Tossing his belongings in the back of a vehicle, he told her, "I'm riding with these guys. They need help setting up a seismic survey at an adjacent station. Then I'll come and help you with the electromagnetic survey." Changing the subject, he asked with a hint of superiority, "Ever used the dipole-dipole technique before?"

Taken aback by his obnoxious question, Donna recalled that Eli had hired her because of her familiarity with the technology. The lawyer had no control over the selection of technicians on the site. The company had requested that they use this crew from an independent geophysical consulting firm.

"That's fine," Donna replied, ignoring his question. "Give me a few minutes. It looks like I left one of my bags at home. It won't take long to retrieve it. Go ahead."

"Oh, okay," the man answered. Glancing down at his clipboard, he sighed in resignation. Then he turned and rejoined his crew. As he climbed into the cab of the other truck, he instructed them to drive on.

Donna watched them until the truck had vanished from view. She did not want the crew to see her clean up the truck. Calling the guard over for assistance, together they mopped up the gasoline spill with some old rags found in his guard booth. She left him to dispose of them appropriately. Then Donna drove the truck to the back of the geophysics building where they kept their own survey equipment. She motioned some men at the dock to help her unload the leaky generator.

"Tell Dr. McClendon that I don't need this generator. The company's crew confirmed that I am doing a dipole-dipole survey rather than a resistivity survey." Pulling a case from the vehicle, she carefully handed it over to the attendant and added, "Also, I don't need this bag of dynamite either. It is for the seismic crew, and they must have put an extra bag in my vehicle. Just let Dr. McClendon know what is going on."

One of the men raised an eyebrow and nodded. The seasoned crew seemed very sloppy with their equipment or else they harbored malice toward the consultant. Acknowledging the risk, he nodded at Donna and lifted the generator out of the truck with the younger man's help. While the younger man safely stored the contents away, he began scribbling notes for Dr. McClendon along with his own notes about what he found in the truck.

"Here is my number here at the storeroom in case you need it," he told her as he handed her a torn slip of paper. Call me if needed. Dr. McClendon won't be back from his survey until tomorrow afternoon."

Donna took a deep breath and determined how to continue from this point. Caught in a bind, she felt reassured that the technicians at the dock watched out for her. She wondered whether she should feign mechanical difficulty with the vehicle and skip this trip altogether. For the moment, she knew that she could get away with separating the extraneous survey equipment from her own survey. She could cite the need for professionalism and safety precautions. The state gave dynamite licenses to only a few geologists specifically for seismic surveys, where a minor explosion simulated the flow of vibrational waves through different rock layers. The measurements could be used to detect underground water, changes in rock formations, or buried tanks of poisonous substances.

In her mind's eye she quickly fathomed the depth of this situation and decided that she needed to keep moving forward. Her thoughts raced to the most sensible solution. If she balked, then she might blow their cover. Before going down the road, she looked at the map. It seemed straight forward enough. Someone from the Environmental Protection Agency promised to be in the area too. She would not be alone. Settling behind the wheel with a sigh, she inwardly knew that she had to force the issue. Running away now would attract attention. The result could betray the entire operation. She drove off with a wave to the men at the shop. Irritated by the intriguing circumstances, she focused on her driving and murmured, "The things we do for science."

This remark kept the situation in perspective for her. Scientific intrigue differed from the cloak and dagger business. She thought about what she had learned through life experience. If she just took it easy and meandered her way through obstacles, then adverse circumstances went away like water on the back of a duck. As a geologist, she could always pass on the survey if needed, though ninety percent of life was just showing up, she told herself. This gave her more room to back out. Geologists operated on geologic time and they often took their sweet time doing surveys, especially if the situation didn't feel right. Donna's thoughts drifted to her friend Carrie, who supposedly pursued studies in Italy. The connection with her friend soothed her in this present terrain. Carrie always found a way out.

The blue truck passed fields of tall coastal grasses and trees dwarfed by the wind-swept environment. At last she came to the survey site about a mile away from the company. A large white truck from the Environmental Protection Agency remained parked along a dirt road. The road led to a densely wooded area, where they parked the blue truck several yards away.

The man with the clipboard stood on the passenger side and wrote down information. Donna stopped her vehicle next to the vacant truck from the agency.

"What took you so long?" the man with the clipboard asked. He had left his position to meet her. Donna noticed his blink and the impatient way he hopped from one foot to another.

Donna didn't respond to his question, the second obnoxious one he had asked that day. "Where is the agency man?" she quizzed him as she began pulling the lengthy dipole wand out of the truck. Silently, she wired it to a measuring device.

"His car was already here when I came. I haven't seen him. He arrived early." The stocky man gestured towards the woods as he spoke.

"Let's go," she said. Searching the field for the agency man, Donna reached out to someone who could document her whereabouts. Her shoulders rose with the tension in the air. An attack could be thwarted by exposing her location.

Donna slipped the measuring device over her head and strapped it around her waist with a belt. She put a new paper tape into the device and handed the lengthy pole to the man to carry beside her. The stocky man stepped back as he stared at the pole that would demand all his attention to carry. The highly flexible pole drooped at both ends. It required concentration to avoid the trees and shrubs, while stepping over rocks and holes in the uneven terrain. This purposeful distraction provided lifesaving potential, while relaxing the tensions in her shoulders.

Within thirty minutes they met the agency inspector. He walked over to them with his hand covering his nose. "It smells over here. Where are your safety masks?" he asked. "I'm going back to get mine."

Donna stopped and examined the data that registered on her ticker tape. The electromagnetic data started to indicate lethal proportions. Like most agency inspectors, this man had a sensitive nose. As a field geologist, Donna had never had developed this talent for sniffing out hazard levels at a waste site. Far from being considered psychic, the best professionals developed pertinent, on-the-job senses. Missing her connection with the agency man, Donna noted the escalation of her own hazardous situation.

"Seems this ticker tape isn't responding too well. Must have gotten wet or something in the truck," she stated, pounding her machine as if it were broken. "I'm going to need to go back to the truck for another roll if this continues," she announced, concealing her eagerness. Donna let another few minutes pass with intermittent thumps on the machine, before she decisively said, "I need to go back for another tape."

The man left holding the drooping dipole rod seemed distracted. "Huh? Oh, yeah sure," he mustered.

Donna witnessed his frantic attempts to regain command of the situation. She glanced at the woods and searched for signs of life. Ready to bolt, she harnessed the power in her leg muscles.

"Listen," he told her after she had returned to the truck and had started to fake a fumble for spare ticker tape. His words were interrupted by a call on his walkie-talkie, which he quickly answered. He nodded as his eyes swirled around the environment, sizing up the situation and agreeing. The man hung-up almost as quickly as he had answered the walkie-talkie.

"Say, they need my help to sort out another survey," he told her in a deflated voice. "Let's finish this tomorrow. I'll meet you here at eight o'clock in the morning."

After hurriedly gathering his things, he hopped in his car and drove away. Donna looked again in the direction of the agency inspector. He had disappeared from her view. She wondered whether the inspector was one of those celestials who traveled through time and seemed to show up at precisely the right moment. If the agency man had been on schedule, she realized that she would have missed him and the crew would have targeted her. Experience had taught Donna to keep an eye open for these people who seem to appear out of nowhere, offering timely validations. The dark side had their matrix and she had her light distractions, connecting her to a divine web, one so fine that many missed it.

Chapter Eight

Appreciate the essence

Of a rock rose

And the earth-bound qualities of the brave

Tune Reference: *Superman*

----Five for the Fighting

DONNA DROVE BACK to the shop at the back of the geophysics building. She left the truck at the entrance to the garage and noticed that none of the regular workers were there. A clean-cut man appeared from the glass-enclosed office and quickly helped her stow the gear. She had never seen him before. Without asking any questions, he offered her the use of the office phone.

Donna called Eli's law firm and left a message with his receptionist. "Tell him I came down with the flu and won't be able to make it back tomorrow."

As if on cue, the clean-shaven man nodded slightly when he overheard her alibi. He informed her, "You can find Dr. McClendon at the training hall."

He ushered her out of the garage and sent Donna on her way. By the time she had walked half a block, Donna realized that she had met another time traveler helping her keep her link with the divine web. It dawned on her that the man at the geophysics building had been a time traveler helping her along the way. Having passed another checkpoint, she confidently hurried to the training hall. Despite the circumstances and harrowing escape, she remained on schedule.

Her thoughts drifted over to Eli as she walked through town. At least this time, she had someone to call for help. Thinking of him centered her somehow. Given the rings of intrigue, he might be in danger. Opening the door to the exercise hall, she dismissed her feelings about him.

"Just in time for class," Dr. McClendon greeted with a mustached grin and folded-hand salute. He noticed that she didn't have the proper attire for class and overlooked the situation without pressuring her with questions. "Here, change into these sweats," he told her, thrusting a tee shirt and sweat pants into her hands. With a wave, he motioned her towards the women's restroom.

As she quietly turned towards the door to change, Dr. McClendon shoved a folded piece of paper in her hands. Reading the flyer from a local art gallery, Donna recognized the featured painting from her parent's living room at home. The scene depicted the clay streets of Mexico. A major aberration in the painting jolted her senses and sent a quiver up her spine. The alteration subtly drawn into the painting could have fooled those unfamiliar with the piece. In the foreground of the sleepy town, a black dog led a woman in a blue cape with a troll behind her. The troll stood out the most, though some might have mistaken it for an inkblot against the sterile clay walls of a Hispanic town---an artist error on an inexpensive painting. However, Donna puzzled over the black dog leading the sad, forlorn woman through the empty city streets. Most street artists didn't paint human subjects behind canine, much less a black dog with a hung head.

"A man outside the training hall wanted to be sure that you got this," Dr. McClendon explained. His hand dove inside his pockets as he stared at the floor of the gym. Casually studying the floor, he waited for an auditory response.

Donna nodded and quickly changed her clothes before returning to the training hall. She gave Dr. McClendon a folded-hand salute and joined the only other person in the room. Her refusal to offer an explanation discouraged those in the room.

"It's going to be a light class tonight," Dr. McClendon remarked. "Donna, please welcome Joan. She is an osteopathic physician from Maine. She has studied with me at the club outside of Searsport."

"Hi Donna," Joan warmly smiled, stretching her slender figure across the wood floor.

Donna smiled in return and followed suit with her warmup exercises. Dr. McClendon continued with his agenda.

"Who is the black dog?" Dr. McClendon asked as he glanced in Donna's direction.

"Is this a rhetorical question?" Donna mused, turning the other away in a stretch.

"Or a Jungian archetype?" Joan interrupted. She stared at the floor while bowing her head over an extended leg.

Dr. McClendon remained unfettered as he focused on his own warmup exercises. "Or a tip-off?" he postulated. "Tell us about your walk in the park with the boys from Brazil?"

"Is this rhetorical?" Donna repeated, recognizing his reference to nazi medical experiments in South America. Putting aside the tensions in the room, she glanced down at the floor as she assumed another pose. Instead of responding, she returned the question. "Are black dogs to be trusted?"

"A popular homeopathic deals with this archetype," Joan interjected. She continued stretching, while deftly shifting the conversation to a more neutral, philosophic stance. Being a physician, she fathomed the stress in the undercurrents of the congenial chatter. "It has to do with the dogs of war or the dog-eat-dog world where the masculine domestic instincts have gone awry." She paused for the information to sink in.

Donna focused intently on her leg stretches as Dr. McClendon sighed into the distance before delivering a blow to the punching bag hanging from the ceiling. Though the sound echoed through the room, the two women ignored the drama. Without flinching, Donna searched Joan's eyes for an explanation.

"Dogs represent the male domestic instincts in Jungian archetypes," Joan added, confident that she had calmed the room and caught their attention. Otherwise the tension between the Viet Nam vet and the woman-on-the-run would have escalated without a productive solution.

"I called-in sick for tomorrow with a case of the flu," Donna admitted. "Eli will have to get the data another way. They want to kill me."

Joan eyed Donna silently, while continuing with her stretches. Now everyone knew what had been bothering the woman-on-run. Joan sensed that the negative cycle had been broken.

"Ever hear of the Civil Air Patrol?" Donna asked. "Some are Search and Rescue units and others are dogs of war."

"Yes, Garrison, the only attorney outside the Warren Commission investigating the JFK assassination talked about it," Dr. McClendon said softly. "It proved a setup for Garrison's star witness. Oswald came from the same outfit, which answered to the same military-industrial complex that owned the Depository and Ling-Temco-Vought or LTV. LTV and Bell Helicopter produced many of the 'Nam war machines. They setup Oswald for his role in the downing of the U2 flown by Gary Powers., This disrupted Eisenhower's peace talks with the Soviets. Oswald had also worked with the U2 planes in Japan, as the armories from World War II were being placed in "Nam and Korea."

"*99 Luftballoons*," Joan commented as she took a punch at an adjacent bag.

With a shrug Donna raised her head and pricked her ears, recalling the tune of 'Luftballoon' a popular environmental song. She shook her head at the complications between those who profited by war and those who preferred peace. Meanwhile, Joan purposely calmed the tensions in the room as she hummed, *Ninety-nine red balloons floating in the summer sky...the war machine springs to life opening one eager eye...*

"I had a dream last night about a man who looked just like the one in the photograph behind you on the altar," Donna remarked, changing the subject. "Other than the fact that he is Chinese, he reminds me of my late grandfather."

"Why?" Dr. McClendon asked out loud. "I brought in this photograph today. It's the first time that it has ever been in the training room." After a moment's reflection, he took the framed photograph from the altar and handed it to Donna. "This is now your grandfather."

Cautiously changing the subject back to the initial topic, Dr. McClendon ventured, "Admiral Byrd operated the Civil Air Patrol. His cousin, owner of the Texas School Book Depository, funded missions. The Admiral worked with the Grays, Nazis, Birchers, Confederates, Vatican, and

Russian underground in places such as Antarctica, Greenland, and the Arctic Circle. The military-corporate-oligarchy financed the expeditions. Some government reports say that the expeditions pertained to aliens."

Shaking her head, Donna ignored Dr. McClendon's deviation. Instead she gazed at the man from her dreams. At the age of 118 years, his face appeared wrinkle-free. Donna chuckled. "This master has a baby face."

Realizing that he would get no further information from Donna, Dr. McClendon continued, "In the lineage, the instructors are called 'grandfather.'"

Donna nodded her understanding. This man did seem very grand and patriarchal. Unlike the apparitions from the dog-eat-dog world, he seemed very human and peaceful.

"Practitioners of the Taoist Ruler possessed a penchant for longevity," he continued. "The grandmother worked at the spindle, which is why the ruler resembles a spindle. Intending to keep her grandsons out of street gangs, she challenged the local authority according to custom. She won, and her grandsons promised to stay out of street fights if she would teach them the Taoist Ruler."

Donna smiled as she thought about a martial arts set created by an elderly woman. She wasn't into punching bags or breaking bricks, but she could get into waving a spindle in the air, especially if it empowered grandmothers.

"Okay," Dr. McClendon declared, abruptly changing the subject again. "Time for Waving Palms. We'll share information later as events unfold. Enough for today."

The small class of three, including the instructor lined up for the exercise. Then the three players assumed a horse stance and circled their arms in the air in deliberate, timed motions. No more words were said or needed. Joan had brought them back on course and their collective energy soothed, strengthened, and balanced their nerves. They emerged from the short exercises as respectful friends, gently saluting and nodding good-byes in the softly-lit studio before venturing into the night for their separate destinations home.

Donna walked up the street towards town. She could not figure out which art gallery had given Dr. McClendon the flyer. Stopping by a phone booth, she placed a call to Eric. She briefly told him about why her project with the lawyer was being put on hold for the time being. After making plans to meet for lunch the next day, Donna left the phone booth and headed back to her apartment. While checking to be sure that she wasn't being followed, Donna climbed the stairs leading to her suite. For the first time today, she felt safe. She glanced at the blackness of the cape before turning her key into the door. Flooding the lights to the apartment with an abrupt flip of the switch, she sighed with relief that nothing in the room had been altered. Soon she fell asleep with the deep, restful contentment that only safety offers.

The next morning Donna returned to the family cottage. There were no signs of life in close vicinity. Everything seemed quiet, practically dead. She unlocked the familiar front door and stepped slowly into the living room. Finding a sense of calm in her trained silence, she walked over to the open window with the beach wind blowing sheer curtains like a bellow. She looked down at the sofa chair near the window and noticed a syringe sticking from its upholstered arm. She almost gasped, but experience silenced her. Donna extracted the syringe from the chair and held it in the light. Squeezing the plunger curiously in the light, she watched a drop of clear liquid escape and drop to the floor. Without anybody that she could turn to for further investigation, Donna inhabited a world beyond the reach of any police or government intelligence agency. The questions remained hers to satisfactorily investigate.

Later she joined Dr. McClendon at the office. Handing her some mail, he told her that Eli wanted to meet with her in a couple of days for some briefing. Donna nodded and glanced at the scribbled forwarding address on the envelopes. The university had forwarded all her information to the geology lab on Woodsport. Donna noticed that one of the envelopes came from Carrie. Her return address was from a hospital near Dallas.

Apparently, Carrie had never made it to Rome and had missed the fateful train bombing. Donna tossed the letter on the desk as she slumped in a nearby chair. As youthful draftee, Carrie's father had belonged to the same Civil Air Patrol group that she had mentioned during exercise class last night. The reasons for Carrie's hospitalization appeared rather vague. The hospital must be torturing her with drugs.

"Good news?" Dr. McClendon questioned, after watching Donna's reaction.

"Relatively," Donna responded. "Though I think one of my friends is being held as collateral for an inherited legacy. She has a good sixth sense and she'll find her way out of it. She's stayed alive this long."

"Great," Dr. McClendon said with a nod. He turned his attention to his own work in the adjacent room. "Great."

Eric picked her up at the apartment later in the evening to take her to Dr. Lorenzo's and Margarette's home.

"So nice to see you again," Dr. Lorenzo beamed when he ushered them in the door. He led them to the table surrounded by the view of the cape. Relaxed in one of the chairs by the picture window, Margarette rose to greet her guests with a warm smile. Meanwhile, Dr. Lorenzo began offering and pouring glasses of wine. The dark opaque glasses twinkled in the candlelight as outstretched arms reached for the containers, before lifting them in the air with a frenzy of words.

"How's it going with the geophysics lab?" Dr. Lorenzo asked between smooth sips from his burgundy glass. Another thought crossed his mind, and he sat his glass firmly down on the table. "Do care you care for bell peppers? Margarette bought some fresh ones at the market today."

"And I have fresh bread too," she said with a smiling sigh, anticipating the aroma of fresh bread served simply amongst intimate friends as if it were the main course itself. With a light nod, she immediately left for the servings.

Moved by their generous warmth, Donna embarked on a light topic. "I've been modeling seismic data for California and it's going well."

Dr. Lorenzo softly pressed the conversation as Margarette entered with a tray of fresh bread and appetizers. "Thank you for joining us tonight."

Donna sat down with Margarette at the table. The darkness enveloping the cape outside the window had started to relax her. "The job with the law firm was cancelled. I don't know where it will go from here."

"Oh," he offered.

Donna stared outside the window and into the darkness. "It's a heavy business."

"Oh," Dr. Lorenzo said again. Eric stared absently at the table. "We have two new physicists at the lab from Russia. They dropped everything in their country and came here never to return to their homeland. They are very serious, and very difficult to get to lighten up."

Donna brightened.

"In our country, we don't take anything seriously," Dr. Lorenzo remarked. We've seen corrupt popes come and go. We adjust."

"And this latest bombing?" Donna questioned, imagining a culture where the people were not fooled.

"Probably the work of left-behind renegade NATO forces," Eric interjected without changing his facial expression.

"Oh, you've read Lyndon LaRouche?" Margarette observed with a soft grin. "In Europe we called him the Malcolm X of US politics."

"Oh," Donna said, slowly drifting into the center of the conversation without knowing it.

"It seems that many of the secret intelligence units from WWII split off into different fractions."

"A relation of Jacqueline Kennedy's stepfather formed the CIA."

"Oh," Donna repeated.

"Kennedy, himself, had been in naval intelligence. He did trade-offs with the Russians at the border in Budapest," Eric added.

"The Russians supported the Union during the Civil War and through two World Wars. Without their support we would have lost. The mystique of the Cold War appears almost whimsical given the history. Just like the rule of the popes..." Dr. Lorenzo trailed off.

Donna just sat back and listened. She wondered where these people were going with this topic. At any rate, she felt that she could relax in the atmosphere.

"We have to know these things because it affects our research. It determines which projects get funded and what is considered important. Might as well be the Italian way. Just ignore it all and do what moves you." Dr. Lorenzo smiled with mild jubilation.

The rest of the table laughed. Margarette smiled knowingly at Dr. Lorenzo. She, unlike no other, seemed to understand his charmed life. He looked appreciatively at her, as if his lifelong charm.

Donna relented. "The latest project at the labs is crazy. This people in the field were really out of it. I watched one technician carry a gun and swirl it around like he had forgotten he had it. The manager just ducked."

"We have a bunch of Manchurian candidates," Eric said glibly.

"Yeah, well the effects reach global proportions. I got a letter from Carrie," she said as she turned towards him. "She's not in Italy. She landed in a hospital near Dallas."

"What!" Eric and Margarette quietly exclaimed in unison.

"She missed the train bombing in Italy," Donna said on a more positive note.

"And the pope's assassination attempt," Eric observed.

"Huh, when did this happen?" Donna questioned the group. Searching their faces, she understood the course of the conversation. "The pope?"

"One of the hazards of being in the field," Eric commented with a light tease. "You miss the news of the world."

"Oh," Donna said. "A hit by the Grey Wolves?"

Dr. Lorenzo nodded, expressing his delight with the dialogue. He elegantly smiled at the spread on the table. "About those global proportions?"

Margarette rose from her chair to get more food, including the main course. She invited Donna to come with her. Donna left the room and followed her. Obviously enjoying Margarette's company, her awestruck countenance tracked the way her hosts intertwined serious topics with casual conversation and mundane activity. The conversation, though sacred, promised no consequence. Such an intimate evening would be respected and remain confidential. Nothing said would go beyond the present candlelit walls protecting them from the dark waters surrounding them on the outside. Noting their reverent demeanor, Donna realized how odd she appeared to the European world. They nonverbally embraced her as if she had the news that they had been waiting to hear.

"Carrie's father had been in the Bay of Pigs. Until the time of the assassinations, they all thought they were on the right side," Donna's voice quietly trailed as she lifted the tray with the chicken on it. Intent on her activity, Donna lifted her head briefly and noticed that Margarette seemed lost in her own thoughts. So she added, "Then it became too late to get out."

Margarette nodded and placed vegetables and grains on several other trays. The moistness in her eyes reflected many convolutions of world events viewed as a neutral Swiss. Donna watched Margarette touch her heart softly. In silent blessing, she lifted the cloak and dagger confusion emanating from the First World War, where one didn't recognize the true enemy until the fatal dagger hit them.

Chapter Nine

Dance to the heart beat of a hummingbird,
To find the innocence of wood nymphs

Tune Reference: *Daisy Jane*

----America

SIDESTEPPING ANY FURTHER discourse with Dr. McClendon, Eli called Donna at the office the next early afternoon.

"Meet me at the Blue Heron," he implored.

Donna agreed without hesitating and he spoke no further. Eli impressed her as he got beyond her usual defenses. He reminded Donna of her cousins in a late night game of flashlight tag, a game he already knew how to play without any questions. Donna thought about his pursuit and a whimsical smirk came to her lips. Realizing that she could almost taste their next rendezvous, Donna shuddered slightly at the way she opened up to him.

Before leaving, she let Dr. McClendon know she planned to meet with Eli for an extended lunch. Raising his head slightly from his notes, he waved her off. Walking across town to the Blue Heron, Donna recalled her fresh start in this town. Only a few months ago, she had met Eric here for a beer and minor discussion. She peered over the familiar blue shutter doors and spied Eli sitting at the same table where she had met Eric. Taking a deep breath, she composed herself and entered the tavern.

Eli smiled at her when she joined him, motioning for her to have a seat as he summoned a waitress over to serve her.

"Would you like something to drink?' he asked, slightly hurried in his manner to subtly convey the impression that he also wanted privacy. Shifting from one foot to the other as she eyed Eric, the waitress acknowledged his silent request. She quickly departed after Donna added her order.

Quickly getting to the heart of the issue, Eli began, "I'm sorry about the situation with the geophysical survey crew."

Ignoring his sentiment, Donna retained her sense of professionalism and businesslike manner. "I have enough data to confirm the presence of extensive hazardous material on the property."

"We sent another crew to the second site this morning," he persisted, folding his hands in front of his chest and looking nervously at the door. "The men were carrying rifles and seemed very disoriented. They appeared just as confused as a hound dog, which had lost a rabbit in a brier patch. They forgot that they carried deadly rifles, and we found them taking aim at each other like little kids with a new toy.

Donna stared aghast at the table and waved a hand across her face, as if she could hide her expression from him. Settling back in her seat, she mournfully looked at the emptiness on the blank wood between them as if a deck of cards had been dealt. To her relief, the waitress appeared with food and drinks. She accepted her deep burgundy glass and quickly sipped her way into a poker face.

Wrapped in his own perplexity, Eli ignored her. Blinking before perusing the menu, Donna observed that he didn't pay anything attention to her. Her shoulders relaxed as she imagined the feast before her. Taking another deep breath, she folded the cover and placed the laminated card aside. She leaned over the table and grabbed a glass of water. Returning her focus to the man in front of her, she clasped her hands and searched his face for clues regarding his feelings on their looming discussion.

He smiled slightly as their eyes met. Shocked by the warmth, she pulled away from his gaze and placed her hands under the table. With an air of subtle resignation, she hopelessly glanced around the room for relief.

"They intended to kill you," he told her rubbing his own hands across his head. He sat back to observe her reaction.

"I figured that out," Donna said facetiously as she tossed off his statement with a shrug. Opting for something more lighthearted, she reached for the glass filled with the plum-red wine. Without lifting the object to her lips, she curled her fingers around the stem as if sizing up its contents before partaking.

Eli winced slightly, touching her hand softly so that she didn't instinctively pull away. Stepping out of trial lawyer mode, he held her firmly with blank, open stares. With a hint of reservation in his voice, he told her, "I interviewed one of the factory employees today."

Donna looked down on the table and grimaced. Eli drew his extended hand toward his chest and continued, "My office did a background check and found that he had been the illegitimate son of Nazi soldier, who had been extradited to the United States after the war. Some of the former German military leaders were placed within the US system by our intelligence network as part of the booty. He consented to provide testimony while under hypnosis."

He leaned back, gauging Donna's placid face. After she raised her head higher, Eli continued, "Apparently his father had planted information into his subconscious to ensure his progeny's financial security. He had a mental list of people associated with his father's organization that spanned all major countries and continents. He named bankers, corporate leaders, government officials, and military officers from both sides of the wars. The witness also provided details of various assassinations, including Franklin Roosevelt's."

Donna leaned back and crossed her arms. She told him, "The military-industrial complex isn't just an American phenomenon." Suddenly relenting as she thought about Dr. Lorenzo and Margarette, she placed her folded arms on the table and casually moved closer. "They sent the leftovers from World War II to northern Viet Nam while they were still fighting the Korean War. Oswald was at the Japanese base near the time of the transports. This indicated the military's cooperation with communists, after headquarters recalled MacArthur. MacArthur had complained of alien warfare."

Eli cocked his head from side to side to make sure that he had heard her correctly. Bowing his head, he sipped his beer in silent reflection, offering a hint of resignation for less than Donna's display. Clutching his beer mug tightly, he eyed her carefully. Softly shaking his head side to side he conveyed the impression that the basis of his entire understanding had just been shattered.

Without offering any sympathy, Donna stated, "No matter the outcome in the Pacific, there existed a mandate for the atomic bomb. The spinoff technologies needed funding."

Eli nodded. His countenance brightened at Donna's persistence and he acknowledged, "This man revealed that Franklin Roosevelt had been slipped a drug that caused his brain to hemorrhage. Apparently this particular type of murder is frequently employed by this international organization."

"*Si, si*," Donna affirmed in the Spanish word for 'yes'. Then she added, "They kidnapped the Lindberg baby to push the WWI pacifists out of politics. The underground associated with the kidnapping rivaled the Kennedy-bootlegging players. Bobby prosecuted the underground because they were a threat to the administrative branch of the government."

Eli smirked. He gulped his beer, while swallowing the worldview of lawless possibilities associated with the culture just south of the border. He perceived Donna's innuendo, which lightened the discussion considerably.

With only a few words, Donna painted a picture of a thousand images with the careful use of a few metaphors. His face showed the thousand thoughts and ideas that crossed his mind as their discussion raced to memories of all the CIA-related coups and revolutions in Mexico, Guatemala, and Panama. The term banana republic validated this casual association between the spoiled fruit of planned assassinations. A company called United Fruit ran bananas through the underground, which employed many agents formerly associated with the JFK assassination such as the former CIA director and the people Oswald owed rent. They considered the ownership of the Panama Canal, the corporations that had built it, the flags that had flown over it, and the same people who still seem to operate it, despite revolutions. Many of the corporations worked with the Nazi company known as IG Farben, which not only supplied the gas for concentration camps but antibiotics for both sides of the war. This company missed being bombed during WWII, and survived the Nazi war trials to form derivative companies that pushed aspirin and genetically-modified substances. Memories surrounding the Bay of Pigs rolled in and crashed in their dialogues like dramatic waves that slowly ebbed away and returned as a tidal missile crisis, rolling into another assassination, or a coup, or exile for a world leader. Not just another assassination, but a coup on US soil, where fired intelligence officials stayed with the mother of the slain president's wife afterwards. The mother-in-law had not only dated Oswald's handler during the world war, but had married the son of the man who started the country's present intelligence agency. Meanwhile, the owner of the depository went on to build another military-industrial complex and profit by the succeeding war.

Eli shuddered, but it only lasted for a brief moment. He looked into Donna's eyes with a sense of relief. He saw someone who understood the game, but refused to play. Her suffering gave her the vision needed to see beyond the cultural myths like Santa Claus and Camelot. Shark, another name for a lawyer, alluded to the fact that truth often required blood, a reality that could not be easily avoided by those with cultural blind spots.

"What else do these people want besides money and power?" he questioned, pressing her further.

Donna stared at him. His gentle, down-to-earth, simple way of assimilating the bottom-line moved her. Eli stepped inside her world with his inquiry, somehow understanding it without fear or trepidation.

"Armageddon," she answered. "Some want to ascend in divine rapture and others just want to inherit the spoils."

"Oh, it's a religious issue," Eli surmised with a light air of disbelief.

"In some ways," Donna replied as her voice trailed. "Joan could answer that question better, though, Dr. McClendon mentioned Grays. This means that the issue has intergalactic proportions."

"Who is Joan?" Eli asked, ignoring the rest. "I'll talk with Larry later."

"Joan studies martial arts with Dr. McClendon. She would be the first to tell you that her namesake, Joan of Arc, worked for the wrong Frenchman."

Which Frenchman was that?" he asked.

"King Charles from Valois, House of Capet," Donna said. "The same group that fought Camelot or Camelon, depending on whether you prefer the myth or the archaeological digs."

Eli relaxed and finished his beer. Donna still had half a glass left, but appeared disinterested in drinking. She stared at the remainder of food on her plate and waved at the waitress for a doggie bag.

"Where does the religious issue come into it?"

"She fought a holy war, where the same financiers funded both sides," she said, shaking her head in mild dismay. "War for the sake of war is a racket, not a religious issue. The planet loses by reckless profiteering. It's all an illusion."

Eli noticed that Donna had stopped drinking as she accepted the doggie bag from the waitress. Leaning over the table, he rushed into his next question. "Where can I find Joan?"

"Through Dr. McClendon," Donna replied as she glanced at the exit sign. "They trained together in the same exercise class. Both are 23rd generation players. I am in the 24th generation."

A sense of desperation and hopelessness flashed across his face. "How about a walk along the beach?" he offered.

Donna brightened and nodded. Rising from her chair, she lifted her nostrils and walked toward the source of the misty salt breeze. The scent lifted the heaviness from her shoulders and she relaxed as she headed outside. Together they left through the doors of the Blue Heron tavern. They paced down the dimly lit street to the edge of the town where a public trail to the beach descended from the road. The heavier, dense air warmed Donna and her countenance beamed. Eli saw the sudden lack of tension in her body. He smiled to himself as he drew his arm over her in a light invitation to accompany him down the sandy path to the melodious surf. Donna skipped slightly under the arch of his arm before he dropped it back down beside him.

"So tell me," he asked just before they reached the surf, "What's a nice girl like you doing in a place like this?"

Donna whipped her body around like a fairy dancing over the waves of sand and quietly laughed, "Guess!"

"No, you tell me," he told her, replying with a slight smile as Donna landed on a log like a twirling gymnast.

Donna shook her head as she began practicing her balance exercises.

Eli put his hands in his pockets and stared out to sea. He quietly cocked his head and listened in the soft breeze for the words that Donna wasn't saying.

"As Abraham Lincoln would say, 'You can fool some of the people all of the time, and all of the people some of the time, but you cannot fool all of the people all of the time,'" Donna told him.

"You are being cryptic," he lightly taunted her.

"No," she insisted, catching her balance on a log and turning around to deeply inhale the sea breeze. "I am one of those who is not so easily fooled. That's why I am here."

"Oh," he said, beginning to take mild delight at the playful turn in their dialogue. He hopped on an adjacent log and began his own balancing exercises.

"OK, for the record," he began, growing serious while intently playing on the nearby log. "Have you ever had memories of violence that you don't understand? Ever had recollections of doing things not under your own volition? Ever awakened in a motel and wonder how you got there. Ever saw a magazine headline about a slain public official and wondered whether you were the one who did it? Or do you understand what is meant by the phrase 'remember to forget?'"

With a small sigh, Donna stepped off the log and took off her shoes before venturing into the small waves on the beach. "No," she said emphatically. "I know what is happening on all levels."

She scooped some of the salty water in her hands and moistened her face to refresh herself.

Eli sat down on the log and stared at her silhouette against the water's edge. "This isn't the first factory where I found evidence of torture and behavior conditioning."

"I know," Donna said nonchalantly.

"I started with one in the late 1970's and the investigation has enlarged exponentially."

"Don't forget academia," Donna added. The waves swirled around her toes and then drifted back. She looked up at Eli and observed his silhouette with the crescent moon behind him. "I don't know the particulars of your investigation, but it fits with what I have come to know to be true."

Donna left the surf and picked up her shoes. She motioned to him that she wanted to start walking off the beach. Nodding his head, he indicated his readiness to join her departure. Without hesitating, Eli began putting on his shoes. Like the tides, the conversation naturally ebbed. Donna remained fluid in her surroundings as if by instinct. She rarely stayed in one place long enough to be found. Donna allowed Eli to hold her hand in his as they journeyed back away from the water's edge. Without a further gesture or word, she kept her distance and he sensed the chasm between them. When they began climbing the steep trail away from the surf. Donna stopped and tossed her shoulders. Dropping his hold, she focused on the path as she thought about her recent decisions. She wanted to live rather than waste time on the pursuit of knowledge for knowledge's sake, intending to avoid unproductive dramas. Though it had not come up yet, she knew that there existed an extraterrestrial component to such enterprises. Donna firmed her jaw as she glanced up the sandy hill toward the dark skies. Her manner conveyed the intention to avoid those situations, which further complicated her life.

"I'll walk you back to your studio," Eli told her before they took another route across town that provided more shadow cover from the moon and street lamps. Pausing briefly to look at him, Donna quietly accepted his demand. He dropped her off at the door to her apartment and waited for her to settle her living area after turning on the lights. Then he quickly waved without a kiss or further formalities, heading back into the night to retrieve his car parked near the Blue Heron tavern.

Deep inside, he discovered that he loved her. Eli did not admit this to Donna, otherwise, he sensed that she would panic and run further from him. His shark-like instincts told him that she belonged in the wild rather than domesticated scene. The freedom in her spirit attracted him. He lived in a world of rules and legalities, whereas she had learned to live by different protocols, ones that were beyond the artificial constraints of a modern civilization. Lawlessness often brought out the real truths in a world gone mad. He craved the truths Donna revealed to him. It gave him much to think about. In his world, analysis proved everything, whereas her world consisted of facts, instincts, and intuition. Even if it took a lifetime, he desired her trust, then maybe her devotion and love, if she allowed it.

Chapter Ten

If flanked by clowns and jokers
Keep to the middle

Tune Reference: *Stuck in the Middle With You*
----Stealers Wheel

ABOUT A HALF hour later, Donna heard a knock on her door. After collapsing on the couch in deep sleep after the escapade with Eli, she awoke with a sudden jolt. Despite the interrupted slumber, she seemed refreshed and hurriedly rose to greet the caller. Though she recognized Eric's heavy knock, Donna peered out the small window to check on the arrival. Alarmed by the cadence of the knock, she swung the door wide open to free his entry from any obstacles. Eric entered the room like a football linebacker, abruptly stopping in his tracks with dramatic gesticulations.

"They shot Reagan and missed," he exclaimed, making as much commotion as he could legally.

Bemused by his antics, Donna relaxed and reveled in his exuberant undertones. Watching what he did instead of listening to what he said, took the heady seriousness out of the situation and helped her think logically. Eric purposely overplayed the emotional, making it universal and commonplace without minimizing the tone. He used it to keep his perspective.

"I must have sensed the operations at the university," Donna remarked. "Maybe it will take the heat off of me. They obviously have bigger fish on their hit list."

"The one who did it dined with the former Director of the CIA."

Donna gulped. "Reagan fed McCarthy's communism with actors from Hollywood."

"Say, let's go bring a bottle of wine to Dr. Lorenzo and Margarette this evening. They hinted they had no plans for the evening. I know they would like to join me in celebrating your reprieve."

Donna donned a windbreaker and a bottle of red Cabernet. A sudden ring from the phone stopped them. Donna answered the phone and spoke briefly, explaining that she had plans for the evening. Then she hung up the receiver and locked the apartment door behind her as they went out.

She told him, "Eli wanted to alert me about the President's near assassination and invite me out to Plymouth Rock this Friday. He feels the need to touch base with the roots of this nation. He asked me to come along."

Donna did not mention anything more about the phone call as they walked across town. Eric hung onto the silence, like a starved individual waiting for the next morsel. For the moment, he dismissed Eli as the topic for conversation. Donna shouldered a particular type of fragility underneath her calmness. Vulnerability often proved her stronger suite as life played out. Though she remained open to new opportunities, she refused to be pushed, especially on matters of the heart. They maintained a respectful silence while enjoying the scenery. A few moments later, Eric and Donna joined their friends at the familiar candlelit dining table looking out over the dark waters of the cape.

"The world is in shock over the death of John Lennon. Now it is the pope and president," Dr. Lorenzo commented in a rich, eloquent voice as he filled the wine glasses. "The pattern is nothing new, the work of another lone, crazy assassin." He added, "Margarette found this article by LaRoche entitled *How the Lost Corpse Subverts American Intelligence* or something like that. It mentioned several professors at your former university, Donna."

Donna skimmed the article that Margarette produced on the table. She suddenly sighed, gracefully dropping her head on her raised right hand, which rested on the table. She recognized names of professors that many of her friends in the undergraduate programs had mentioned. It seemed the entire academic program had been designed to drive home one undeniable point. They purposely wanted the students to believe that it was impossible to know anything.

Rubbing her forehead, Donna glanced at a yacht making its way across the cape with only a headlight. *How do you know?* Questions of her friends and acquaintances in other graduate programs echoed through her head. Answers had evolved after the Civil War with various occult groups stemming from the remains of the Confederacy. Some fractions went on to raise mayhem in white robes and others donned academic ones. At some point in the hierarchy, they swore allegiance to the 'illumined one', the talking serpent from a biblical garden. They placed as the head of their organization, a reptilian, someone they still listened to after all these years. LaRouche called the present-day network 'beasts' or 'synarchists.' Others within the organization, such as the Carlist professor who had smuggled fascists for Franco, referred to themselves as monarchists or illumined ones. The act of spreading poison like an unnatural, rabid snake served their purpose.

"Eric, remember the 'Dance of the Continents' at the geology department picnics?" Donna asked, glancing at Eric across the table.

He beamed at her. "After a few beers, we all became knowledgeable on the subject. Dr. Freeman divided the party into two land masses and one would dance toward the other. With a little magma, a few erupted like volcanoes."

"Yes, I remember watching the bodies of land masses coming together with Dr. Copperstone's wife. She came up the departmental quote: 'Plate seduction leads to orogeny, a mountain building event.' Actually, the *Dance of the Continents* is the name of a book required for stratigraphy class."

Margarette grinned at the joke, but seriously asked, "What is stratigraphy?"

"It is one of my specialties," Donna replied. "It is the study of rock layering or stratification."

"As Albert Einstein said," Dr. Lorenzo surmised, "The most incomprehensible thing about the Universe is that it is comprehensible."

"So it is with rock layers. We can figure when and what was deposited, and when it moved and how it got that way," Eric rejoined.

"The book is amazing," Donna insisted. Embarking on a discourse, she elaborated, "It assumes a philosophical approach to something as concrete as rocks and proves that you can know these things. Now I am using electromagnetic data to verify the stratigraphic maps that were made in the 1950's. All rock layers have a unique resistivity value. As a result, we can measure more precisely where one layer ends and another begins. Before geophysical data, all geologists relied on the philosophical approach, which I am finding approximates the electromagnetic data. The author of *Dance of the Continents* parallels the constructs of this university's unknowing philosophy, except he tells you that you can figure things out."

"In other words, you can get to the truth without getting lost in some Hegelian dialect," Margarette mused.

"What do you mean?" Dr. Lorenzo smiled as he spoke in a soft velvet voice.

Margarette shyly nodded at Donna and encouraged her to explain. Donna leaned back in her chair and reflected for a moment, trying to grasp at the meaning that Margarette had sensed inside her. She explained, "My undergraduate friends often talked about Hegel as they studied for their Philosophy classes. Hegel believed that two dynamics in the universe opposed each other." Pausing for a moment, she glanced at Eric for some reassurance as she bridged the western and eastern hemispheres. Sensing his encouragement, she continued, "Unlike the harmony of yin and yang in Asian thought, these polar opposites are incompatible. Instead the dynamics play out like two fighting banty roosters, where the wear and tear of the interaction seems necessary for evolution. My friend Carrie disliked the idea because she saw how it kept everyone in a *Catch-22*, an endless struggle."

Donna hesitated for a second and curiously looked at Margarette before resuming, "It is like the Democrats versus the Republicans, or the communists versus the fascists, which wastes valuable time and resources."

Chapter Eleven

Life is more than a chessboard

Walk away from the match

If you really want to play

Tune Reference: *Sparks of the Tempest*

----Kansas

"WHAT ABOUT YOUR friend?" Margarette asked gently, urging Donna towards a conclusion.

Caught by Margarette's persistence, Donna delved further on the subject. "My friend refused to get trapped in the undertow of conflicting thoughts and ideas. She wanted to get to the truth of the matter and move forward rather than get lost."

Margarette nodded and moved back in her chair, having finally heard the answer she had been waiting to hear.

"Ah yes," Dr. Lorenzo lightly echoed.

"Harrington, the author of *Dance of the Continents,* points out that rocks must be studied 'as is' or in context," Eric remarked.

"This is what Carrie talked about when she stated that context defined the truth," Donna added. "The content in our case would be 'rocks', and we learn the truth about how they got there by examining the context in which they are arranged."

Dr. Lorenzo raised a minor point. "So how does geology deal with uncertainty? In physics, we even have a principle of uncertainty."

"All you need is one percent," Eric chimed. He had barely passed undergraduate physics and eagerly divulged any information that he could remember.

Taken aback by the profundity of Eric's interjection, Dr. Lorenzo gleamed. Speaking in a low voice, he said cautiously to Margarette, "In quantum physics, change is initiated by the most modest circumstances."

Margarette nodded her minute understanding and sought further elaboration from Donna.

"Well, geologists have adventures with unconformities," Donna confessed. "We can find the modest circumstances in the stratigraphy."

"Like when the Bermuda schist hits the alluvial fan," Eric said with a laugh.

"He had Dr. Copperstone laughing so hard with that allusion that he almost fell off the formation," Donna recalled, waiting for Dr. Lorenzo and Margarette to finish chuckling. "Did he ever finish the lecture?"

"Nope," Eric said, while still waving his hands in the air to represent the moving rock layers. Then he laughed, recalling that field trips, like rock layers, did not always go as planned. He sipped his wine with a delighted grin as if to say, "Oh well."

The conversation at the table assumed a lighter note, which naturally concluded the evening. After saying brief good-byes, Eric and Donna walked outside and into the night. Passing a wooded grove, they stopped to listen to the sound of a sharp object tapping a hole in a piece of wood.

"Donna, its a red-headed woodpecker drumming into that tree. Look, you can see his beak and feathers in the moonlight."

Stopping to stare at the figure perched overhead, Donna peered into the night. In contrast to the flutter of the hummingbird, the rhythm echoed consistently and pierced the shadows of the cape. She strained to get a closer look at the bird's features. A section of the moon emerged from behind a cloud and lent greater light on the terrain.

"He's all there, dressed in black and white," Donna remarked, as the added light contrasted the colors of the woodpecker's feathers. "This woodpecker has a brilliant red mantle."

Awestruck, the two friends studied the bird for a moment. Eric shook his head and gazed at the sandy loam beneath his feet. Donna noted his reaction and watched him. Steadying his gaze on the street lamps of the city in the distance, he motioned for Donna to quicken the pace and they hurried back to their homes.

A few days later, Donna met Eli in the parking lot near the security guard. He got out of his lemon-yellow Carmen Ghia when he saw Donna. After putting in some early hours modeling more seismic data, she left work early to join him on the venture. He waved and nodded a greeting before going around to the passenger side to open the door for her. Donna slid into the bucket seat, before watching him swiftly move back around the car and into the driver's seat. With a few deft maneuvers of buttons and stick shifts, he backed the car out of the space and turned onto the main road. Taking a deep breath, she sensed her attraction to this good-looking man, who did not mince words when he had an investigation on his mind. As he shifted gears and accumulated speed on the two-lane highway, Donna shuddered when she imagined him speaking in the court. He could procure silence as well as use his words like a knife.

They made their way to Nantucket in the easy, comfortable quiet of the morning. Donna sensed a million questions between the two of them, but neither of them broke the freshness that came with early-morning dew. In light of the previous evening encounter, verbal communication appeared stale. The moisture dripped off the rolling coastal fields and hung in the breeze, permeating their skin and nostrils until the wetness saturated their awareness of the other. Further up the road, the grassy fields gave way to delicate, timid forests tinted with leaves that were just beginning to change for the season. At this junction, Eli interjected a few words.

"Ever seen Plymouth Rock before?"

Donna noticed that the bright cadence of his inquiry seemed to fit the emerging scenery, feeling simultaneously embracing and uplifting. She replied, "No, I haven't. One of my friends claims the first governor of Plymouth as an ancestor." Donna smiled as she reflected on her relationships. "I seem to be in the middle of it all. My neighbors back home were descendants of John Smith. Joan Standish, the osteopath from McClendon's class, her father's name is Miles Standish III. My friend, Eric Collins, is related to the Collins Family. I'm surrounded by descendants."

"Pilgrims?" Eli questioned as he turned down a narrow road lined with a thick forest.

"Rebellion is apparently in the blood. The leaders of the pilgrims were dissidents. England tried pushing them to Holland, but they became too vocal to ignore. In Holland, they had their own printing press. So it was either kill them or put them to work in the new world. Sorta like white slavery or internment."

Eli drove to the entrance of Plymouth Plantation as they spoke. He parked and they both got out of the car, surveying the wooden posts surrounding the entrance to the park. Together, they walked to a plaque marking the entrance. The description included a quote from Samuel Eliot Morison, who deemed the pilgrims the 'spiritual ancestors of all Americans.'

"They received the title because they were the most thankful to be here," Donna mused.

Eli glanced at her and chuckled slightly, taking her hand in his as they entered the park. They followed a winding path through a thick forest and made their way to the Visitor's Center, where they found an extensive display of medicinal herbs used both by the pilgrims and natives.

"Joan would be delighted," Donna commented. "These are the same botanicals that she mentions in class. She works with an herbalist in Maine."

Eli examined a few descriptions of the botanicals on display and thoughtfully nodded, absorbed by the richness of the pilgrims' natural world. Then he glanced at the rays of sunlight flickering through the forest path and motioned Donna forward to a replica of the pilgrims compound. The compound consisted of rows and rows of tiny thatched huts surrounded by fenced yards separating livestock from gardens. On the hill overlooking the huts stood a fort with portholes for munitions. The plaque on the walls of the fort said this was where the pilgrims held their religious services.

"Sorta reminds me of a Celtic training hall," Donna remarked, while meandering through the wooden pews inside the enclosure. "They pray where they fight. Sometimes they pray when they fight."

Eli brightened and laughed softly with her incisive perceptions uniting these two diverse worlds that arose almost at the same time in history. He peered through one of the munitions openings in the wall and noticed the heavy layer of dark storm clouds moving into the area. "I have never thought of the pilgrims as dragon flyers," he admitted. "There are more places I want to check out before the incoming storm disrupts my investigation."

Having glimpsed the gathering clouds, Donna instinctively moved on. "I want to get on overview. We still haven't found the boat or the rock."

She hurried out of the wooden structure with Eli and raced down the path as a few hard raindrops sped them on. Once they reached the *Mayflower* replica, Donna took a step back and eyed the scene. On her right was a giant boulder with a fence around it. The rock, presumed to be the rock that had steadied the Pilgrims, resembled glacial till, a remnant from the various ice ages that had taken hunks off mountains further north and left them stranded in the terrain when the ice melted. Sizing up the scene, Donna commented, "I know a Boston geologist who can pick up any rock fragment and name the rock formation from which it came."

Tossing her head at Plymouth Rock, she opted for a quick board of the *Mayflower*, which amounted to an oversized wooden bucket. Eli followed her lead and bought tickets for the ship. They ambled past slow-moving sightseers on the boardwalk and ignored the monologues of costumed players reenacting insulting scenes from the pilgrims' journey. Below the hull, Donna stopped and stared at the area designated for the pilgrim travelers. Nothing more than a dimly lit stall, the voyage would have discouraged the faint of heart or weak of spirit. Most of the people she knew today would have suffered a mental breakdown on the trip. She noted that the quarters for the ship's crew seemed luxurious by comparison.

Eli paused briefly beside her, before resuming his sketchy wanderings elsewhere. He seemed almost bored with the exhibit. Taking a deep breath before leaving the site, Donna climbed the narrow stairs as streaks of sunlight managed their way through the clouds. She called to Eli and they left the schooner almost as quickly as they had boarded. At the edge of the national park, they both stopped at one of the exhibit signs and began reading it as if trying to glean new significance from what they had just experienced. A voice from one of the costumed players could be heard nearby. As they studied the sign, Donna and Eli could not help but eavesdrop on the lecture.

"Almost half of the pilgrims died the first winter. They buried the dead at night so that the Native Americans could not see how many they had lost. They wanted to inflate their numbers to ward off attack. They buried them over on that south hill," the guide said as he pointed toward land.

Eli and Donna looked up from the billboard and stared at the ominous hillside. They stepped back and paused for a moment. Donna questioned rhetorically, "Didn't the natives consider this area their vacation summer home?" She took his hand as they headed for a deli across the street. "The pilgrims came with the shoot-first-and-ask-questions-later mentality. They must have been totally freaked by the native's scalping rituals, especially after fleeing for their lives from England. Let's see, we have honorable, friendly little Indian war scalpel meets down-to-business, post dark-ages musket. You can see how miscommunications occurred," Donna decided. "It is amazing that they were able to sit down and eat at the same table for Thanksgiving, a total miracle."

Eli shook his head and chuckled. "There's nothing like connecting the terrain to the facts." Turning to face Donna, he observed, "I can see why you specialized in stratigraphy. It changes history to define the context of events."

"Reality check," Donna agreed. She gazed at the landscape as she thought about what she understood about the refined world of law and order, with deference to the race that had written it down first and who possessed the greater missile power. "Yep, the whole irony of the story is that the pilgrims came to envy the native's ways," Donna continued, while they crossed the street and waved-off motorists. "I suspect they secretly wanted to run around half-naked too, and have summer vacation homes complete with food stores to be stolen by desperate white folk."

Eli interrupted Donna briefly to obtain her order for lunch. After opting for a fish sandwich and a dark beer, Donna continued to think out loud. "No wonder they threw a Boston tea party a hundred and fifty years later. Eventually, the pilgrims came around."

Realizing that he had caught a live one, Eli ushered Donna to a nearby table away from public earshot. After settling down comfortably, he leaned towards Donna and pushed a dark beer towards her. Freeing himself from the mass-programmed history of the nation, Eli dove deep inside this young woman's thoughts.

"Well, you know that Benjamin Franklin and John Adams consulted the Iroquois Confederacy on how to set up the new government," Donna recapitulated, while picking the onions out of her sandwich before taking a huge bite.

Dumbstruck, Eli watched her. Falling in love with this attractive, blond revolutionary sitting across from him, he listened attentively. He shuddered at the endless river of fact and context. Making a conscious decision to surrender himself, Eli dropped his head on his raised hand and almost began swooning. He started to gulp his beer methodically.

"You know that John Adams and Benjamin Franklin slept together and had an argument over whether to leave the window open for the night air. Franklin considered night air healthy. They were on their way to visit the Iroquois confederacy and neither wanted to get sick," Donna resumed, sipping her beer, while making sure that Eli partook.

When she watched him take a swig, she continued, "Everyone slept together without sexual innuendo. At the stagecoach junctions, they put five people cross-wised over the bed. Men and women separated, for puritanical reasons, of course, all strangers in the same bed, waiting for the same stagecoach. It couldn't happen today."

Eli ordered another dark beer for them both. He pushed his own glass toward her to loosen her tongue.

Donna refused his and accepted her second beer. She quit speaking after another gulp and blinked. Forgoing the meandering currents of the world, she leaned back in her chair and eyed him with suspicion. Eli evaded her stare and focused on his own mug and sandwich.

"Let's go climb the hill and visit the pilgrim cemetery, the one where they put those who survived the first winter," Donna tested Eli. With a sigh Donna rested her chin on a raised fist, which the table supported at her bent elbow. She added, "The burial ceremony must have been similar to the Universalist church of today or Unitarians, which apparently replaced the earlier Anglican church."

"Let's go," Eli agreed. The alcohol content of his beverage affected him as he left the table. A slight swagger betrayed his lack of control. Donna left a tip on the table before they left. Then she beckoned him to ascend the steep uphill climb to the old cemetery.

"I don't usually visit cemeteries, but since they are the deceased ancestors of my friends, I don't mind the excursion," Donna remarked once they had reached the top of the hill of the first gravesite. Unlike the early covert cemetery on the south hill, this formal cemetery overlooked the town and Nantucket Bay. The rugged hike discouraged feeble tourists. As a forgotten cemetery, several of the graves appeared neglected with fallen or cracked tombstones. Some of the stone tablets hid behind tall grass, evidently out of the lawnmower's reach. The plots had been laid out before power-generated yard care arrived centuries later.

Eli followed Donna around the hillside as she looked for the names of forebears that she knew. The arrangement of the graves and the dates on the tombstones, along with the descriptions left by the survivors, told the story. Though life had been short and difficult, the pilgrims considered living a triumph, similar to the achievement of climbing the steep hillside, which would have been even more difficult as a funeral procession. The final resting place of the ancestors provided a view of the seafaring activities of Nantucket Bay rather than the daily struggles on the plantation. The last resting place faced England from the heights of a distant, peaceful hill.

From the simple stories carved on the tombstones, they learned that the children of the pilgrims had not carried out the peacekeeping vision of their parents. The offspring had eventually stooped to cloak-and-dagger tactics against their perceived enemies instead of diplomacy. Despite this, all had been forgiven on the hill. England had sent both ruffians and idealists to the new world. Not everything could be worked out and not everyone had a sense of ethics or self-control. It became clear from the arrangement and descriptions on the markers that those who stayed within the community loved each other with a deep affection, both sincere and timeless. Bradford's wife had drowned while the *Mayflower* docked in the harbor, and they had left behind their young son in Holland. He later married a widow with two sons and had three more children together. Two of the three had died very young. At some point, the pilgrim church broke in two, when businesspeople replaced the sociopolitical refugees. The description on Governor Bradford's tombstone advised: *What our forefathers with so much difficulty secured, do not basely relinquish.*

By the second generation, the separatist mission of the pilgrims had perished, giving way to the Puritans, who chose to purify the Church of England rather than separate from their original country or religion. They preferred to work within the system. Once the colony near Provincetown stabilized, the differences separating the groups won out. This fractured the former community. The climb up the hill and this revelation sobered Donna to an abysmal depth that would have been cumbersome has it not been tempered by two beers. Donna left Eli to his own conclusions as they journeyed down the hill in silence. Somewhere along the way the spirit of the children had been broken by the harsh realities to the point where they eventually joined the ruffians, regardless whether the motivation concerned greed or survival. In this case, the motivation did not seem to matter. This history set the stage for the next four hundred years. Although the country had eventually separated from England during the American Revolution, there remained factions within that wanted to continue working within the English system, complete with all its cloak-and-dagger relations and politics. This is how, Donna surmised, the descendant of a visionary diplomat like Governor Bradford could be deeply involved with the black operations securing the nation to its former colonial system that encompassed the globe in an empire. The pilgrims had spiritualized a rock when they first landed. Now that rock invoked world fame as a symbol of solidity and steadfastness, marking the first step towards the claim of a nation concerning its 'natural rights'. Now she had just seen the writing in another lesser-known rock, the granite tombstone marking Bradford's grave. Even if the people didn't survive, the rocks carried the message forward. Donna danced a little in the air with the stratigraphic insights.

"It is all in the rocks," Donna observed. She smiled at Eli once they reached the main street in front of the Plymouth Rock.

"Why am I not surprised?" He grinned before calling attention to the distant lightning bolts over the Atlantic.

The skies reminded her of Fourth of July fireworks. She studied the dark bellowing clouds and lightning streaks for signs of the extraordinary.

"It's coming in fast," Eli observed, "and I don't want to drive. Let's check out the local pilgrim museum."

The museum around the corner proved just as drab and stark as the austere lives of the people it portrayed, which would have been enough to drive anyone into commerce unless they nourished a deep love of the outdoors or fostered the spirituality of a monk. Meanwhile, the clouds moved closer and the storm settled in the town. Eli and Donna marveled at the heavy rain pelting the windows laced between exhibits. The streaks of light and blasts of thunder interrupted the dense atmosphere of the museum exhibits. Elevating the surrounding consciousness, the storm offered hope in an intrusive manner that could not be ignored. Drawn out of the museum by this subtle, enlightened sense, they met each other at the entrance under the porch eaves. While staring at the buckets of water dumping from the skies, Eli and Donna pondered their departure.

"Let's wait out the storm at that coffeehouse overlooking the bay," Eli suggested. "I noticed that they had a little fireplace where we can dry-off. We'll need it, after we get wet trying to get there."

Donna agreed and together they ran from the porch. They covered their heads with whatever thick travel brochures they happened to be carrying.

They scurried from awning to awning and ducked between adjacent buildings to make their way through the storm with the least amount of exposure to the elements. Eventually they slipped inside the door of another redbrick building and climbed the old wooden stairs leading to the coffeehouse on the second floor. Surprised by the number of vacant seats in the room, they momentarily froze near the entrance. Most tourists had fled back to their hotel rooms or found refuge in the restaurants at street level.

They found a small table providing a view of the bay and Mayflower replica. Donna ordered a cup of chamomile tea while Eli ordered mint tea. Mighty booms emerged from the skies and permeated the confines of the building. Flashes of light spontaneously erupted from within the room.

"The ancestors speak!" Donna announced, waving her arms in the air as if to contain the boldness of their statement.

Blinking, Eli acknowledged the extraordinary presence and nodded wide-eyed as more flashes of light darted under their gaze. He felt that he had never seen anything like it before, though Donna appeared reassured by the dramatic display of light and sound. "I think we have more than just pilgrims here."

"Well, they did win in the end," Donna said as a flash of light emphasized her words.

Together, they silently read a caption from a brochure. The Puritans were done in by their own internal witch hunts and faded away. By the time of the American Revolution, a third of the population adamantly refused to continue working within the system. They had support from some of the world's greatest minds from Mozart to Leibniz, the father of Integrated Calculus. Da Vinci, the one who first proposed 'natural rights' stated that humanity should be naturally free, and a mathematician called Leibniz freed himself from Newton's analysis. Enslaved to the monarchs and religious orders, the Renaissance artists sought freedom. They dreamed about it and this distant continent across the water provided an opportunity.

Donna commented, "So we have the illumined ones who give us hell, whereas spirits like the Thunder People open up the heavens, literally."

A roll of thunder echoed loudly across the bay as Donna finished her point. Grinning as she glanced at the overhead skies, she added, "Or least, make the heavens more accessible."

Eli did not argue. Quietly, he turned towards the sky with an expression of amazement and hope.

Chapter Twelve

Get over it

Deal

And quit apologizing

Or making excuses

Tune Reference: *Sister Golden Hair*

----America

DRAWING ELI BACK into the conversation, Donna challenged, "Your focus filters out the spiritual side of things, even when you are investigating people who have been victimized by mind control. You still ultimately arrive at the group who leads them all. Now this dark group has its own spiritual organization into other worlds or other dimensions, regardless whether these souls operate solely from the reptilian portion of the brain."

Softer thunder rolled across the skies as more flashes of light streaked around the room. Encouraged by the calamity, Donna crossed her arms as she leaned back in her chair. More streaks of light filled the room. The lightning bolts missed the couple by a mere foot.

Eli noticed the lightning flash nearly two feet from his right foot. He lightly tossed Donna a panicked look. Confused and bewildered by the seemingly lethal streaks surrounding them, he searched their surroundings for an explanation.

"Some thunderstorms are just atmospheric," Donna observed with a sigh. "They have a unique beat."

"Lightning strokes can be lethal," he retorted, searching the room for cover.

Ignoring the helpless look on Eli's face, she continued, "The ones with dry flashes of lightning that originate from within the room itself are extraordinary." She quieted as Eli arrived at his own conclusions.

"So how long are they going to keep us in Plymouth?" he questioned.

"Until they've made their point."

Hearing her words, Eli rolled his eyes as he cocked his head. "Are you referring to the synchronicity found in Jungian Psychology?"

"Yes," she answered with a shrug. Raising one eyebrow, she suggested, "Be mindful of your symbols. This is where the pilgrims went wrong."

Donna dismissed Eli's fear with a wave of her hand, before savoring the warmth of her beverage. Both quietly sipped their tea as the rain turned into a light shower. They heard the thunder move into the distance, which extended the time between the flashes of light and the sound. Any sense of the extraordinary diminished, leaving only a few occasional rolls and streaks as a reminder.

"I had not realized that the pilgrims had gone wrong. Let's make a break for it before the Thunder People decide to come back for another lecture," Eli suggested after he had finished tea. Having composed himself in the absence of the extraordinary, he ended the conversation abruptly.

"Let's go," Donna agreed, rising from the table. She raced for the door ahead of him. Twirling around to face Eli as she pushed it open for both of them, she wryly remarked, "While, we still can."

Eli's expression softened with Donna's sense of humor. They exited the shop and located the Carmen Ghia on the side of the road. Pendants of crystal water ran down the hood of the car and on their heads as they opened the car door. Hopping into their seats, they scanned the horizon for an upcoming storm. Eli started the car and drove onto the highway.

The vehicle moved forward, gathering speed. Eli shook the water off his head as he thoughtfully gazed at the highway. "It's like coming out of the Land of Oz or Oswald with just a click of the heels." There is no place like the natural world."

"There's always Kansas," Donna remarked.

Hesitating to reply as he shifted gears, Eli glanced at her. Smiling at the illusion, he pointed at a rainbow in the mists. They spoke no more words to each other. Lost in each other's thoughts, they never noticed the silence connecting them so profoundly. After arriving in Woodsport, Eli dropped Donna off at the parking lot adjacent the geophysics building.

"Thank you for you help," Eli told her as he opened the car door. "I'll call you after I recheck my schedule. There's more to discuss."

Donna smiled in reply and ran back to the office to retrieve some things that she had left earlier. She watched Eli drive-off and turn the corner. The moment provided closure for the type of day that seemed to go on forever.

Some days passed one day at a time, and others passed like two or three at a time. Glancing at the afternoon sun, Donna opened the locked door to the office. She found the place vacant, and took the time to examine her workplace free from distractions. After several hours, the graying daylight cast shadows in the uninhabited room. With a hint of weariness, she gathered her things and walked back to her studio apartment.

After climbing the stairs to the studio apartment, she opted for a view of the beach before entering. The swirl of waves and gray mist captivated her as usual, except this time she sensed the waves calling to her in their soft rolling thunder. The sound resonated with the storm at Plymouth and rejuvenated her.

Later, in the early evening, Donna ventured down a new path to the beach. More secluded than the main one she had taken with Eli, the trail proved easier to follow than the one by the family cottage. Glancing in the distance, she spotted a man standing up to his mid-calves in the surf. He had rolled up his long pants and stood sideways looking out to sea. As she got closer to the figure, she recognized Eli. Stopping in her tracks, she hesitated to approach him or betray her location by calling to him. He had not seen her, being absorbed in his own thoughts. Alone in his world, he danced with both the surf and sky, which appeared indistinguishable in mutual grayness except for the white foam on the swift moving water.

Donna often met people in synchronous moments. Members of her family appeared unexpectedly as if an invisible thread held them together. The connection protected from anyone who might be remotely tracking them, such as black military operatives. Her ancestors had used this sense of radar and cosmic timing to command vast armies without the use of walkie-talkies. Communication with Celtic relatives at family reunions had a nonverbal, intuitive connection, which deepened ties profoundly.

Donna felt her heartbeat quicken as she continued walking to meet him. Close to her favorite spot on the beach, he returned where they had played and talked on the logs earlier. With every step forward, she entertained a sense of commitment. He never noticed her arrival. She could turn around and walk away without being seen. Oblivious to her presence on the beach, he lingered in residual moments instead.

Chapter Thirteen

When your dreams arrive

Reel them in

Tune Reference: *Make It With You*

----Bread

TAKING A DEEP breath, Donna straightened and confronted Eli. When she stood almost square with him, he turned and faced her. Being early in the evening, the setting sun cast diminishing hues of gray across the beachfront. Water spots shone on his slacks and dress shirt, sometimes glistening in the occasional silver streaks of the hazy sun. Eli's tousled blonde hair dripped water from the spray and he reminded Donna of a soggy, wet puppy.

"I came to listen," Eli told her. He took a few steps toward her so he could be heard over the waves. Then he stood his ground in the swirling currents wrapped around his ankles. Almost toppling head-over-heels in the surf, Eli steadied his balance. "I am surprised to see you," he began. "I heard the surf call and came to pay a visit, after phoning my receptionist." Pausing for a moment, he collected his thoughts as he stepped closer. "My associates at the plant found the survey crew slinging pistols absentmindedly around the factory. The employees and owner merely ducked under the tables. The entire place is out of its mind," he admitted. Looking at her directly, he questioned, "And you called in sick with the 'flu'?"

Donna remained silent, refusing to entertain his line of questioning. Shaking her head, Donna started to back away and eyed her exit route. Raising her shoulders, she stopped in her tracks and stared at the sand beneath her feet. The wind blew tiny grains of quartz over the ground. Rising no higher than several inches, the blown particles scurried across the terrain, far from previous landings.

"You seem more aware of these operations than I am," he confessed, luring her back. "You may be a dedicated geophysicist but your life encompasses much more than rocks. Who are you? Why would they make such an effort to kill you, before even knowing the results?"

"I see through their schemes," Donna surmised. Sitting down on the log, she covered her face with her hands to screen her vision. The warmth of a sudden sunburst disarmed her and she lowered her arms. She felt herself being pulled by this man as if being sweep up unexpectedly in an undertow. He had found his way inside her thoughts, after arriving at her sacred spot on the beach.

Eli walked towards her and sat down beside her. Like a shark, he went for blood. "How did this happen?" he asked her gently, continuing to cut to the truth.

Donna looked at Eli like he came from outer space. "Why blame me?" Drawing lines in the sand around her feet, she added, "My father served in the military. Didn't yours?"

"He went in the National Guard."

"My father served as an elite member of the military-industrial-complex," Donna said with a sigh. "The Black Dogs protect US terrain."

"Like Black Ops?"

Donna stared out to sea. She continued, "My father saw the war in Korea, before the complex developed. He helped with the investigations, but soon too many people started getting killed off and they ended in confusion, more or less. Those that remain in the Black Dogs cannot get out without putting their lives and families at risk. The military-industrial-complex uses their families as collateral, endlessly torturing them to control those left in the operations. My friend Carrie somehow managed to survive an occult Rite 33 at a tender age. She has been pursued all her life. Her father is in deep, because he disobeyed orders to shoot Jacqueline Kennedy. He exercised free will during a military operation."

"So he is a hero to those wishing to break the mind-control. The Black Dogs see through the schemes. Not everyone has eyes wide shut."

Eli stared out to sea with Donna. She continued, "An occult Rite 33 is the spiritual equivalent of a modern-day crucifixion. It's an ancient rite associated with King Solomon's corrupt temple. The ritual assassination spiritually annihilates a soul. All these horrific tools were developed right underneath Solomon's nose."

"So what is your stake in this whole thing?" Eli asked, moving closer to her on the log.

"My ancestors came from Europe," Donna explained. "That explains it. They aren't corporate pawns."

"I want to hear about the Irish," Eli quipped.

"They have been fighting the British or remnant Roman Empire since the 1100's," Donna replied. "My ancestors led the northern and southern kingdoms. After avoiding the Irish Potato Famine, they fled and intermarried on this continent. The British Parliament orchestrated the famine as a form of genocide. Naturally, we are talking to the descendants of the pilgrims these days and communing with their ancestors. It is a battle for the planet, like the

intergalactic wars of ancient Egypt."

Chapter Fourteen

To live on the planet

You are going to have to

Laugh, sing, fight, and dance

Tune Reference: *Rock 'N Roll Fantasy*

----Bad Company

DONNA PULLED OFF her shoes and socks and waded knee-deep into the waves. She jested, "Aye, my lad, you must understand the Irish by their songs. Just like geologists, the land brings them to tears."

As the waves endlessly crashed on the beach, Donna told him about an old Irish tune by Tommy Makem. In the song, the elders refer to their land as jewels. They voiced their grief and dissatisfaction with the wars, death, plunder, pillage, and starvation that robbed them of their youth and treasure. The song offers hope that future generations will be free to restore the land.

Eli listened to her words and understood. His history professors had always told him to go back to original sources, which consisted of the journals, songs, and testimonies of the people that had been there. He impatiently stood on the shore and waited for her to continue. Donna scooped some of the salty water in her hands, before splashing it on to her face. Then she stared into the gray horizon, before resuming, "My great-great grandfather came to this country just in time to join the Irish Volunteers on the side of the Union. His regiment song referred to the fight of their forefathers in 1798. After the elders died protecting Ireland, they cut their losses and fled to this country to live. When the descendants saw that the South had betrayed the nation to the same foes, they enlisted with the Union to protect their lands. The ancestors valued firm ground over gilded lifestyles. Their descendants fought to preserve law and order from reigning chaos."

Staring out to sea, she recited an old, tune from public domain.

My name is Tim McDonald, I'm a native of the Isle,

I was born among old Erin's bogs when I was but a child.

My father fought in Ninety-Eight for liberty so dear;

He fell upon old Vinegar Hill line an Irish volunteer.

Then raised the harp of Erin, boys, the flag we all revere.

We'll fight and fall beneath its folds like Irish volunteers!

When I was driven from my home by an oppressor's hand,

I cut my sticks and greased by brogues and came o'er to this land.

I found a home and many friends and some that I love dear;

Be jabbers! I'll stick to them like bricks and an Irish volunteer.

Then fill your glasses up, my boys, and drink a hearty cheer,

To the land of our adoption and the Irish volunteer.

Now when the traitors in the South commenced a warlike raid,

I quickly then laid down my hod, to the divil went my spade!

To a recruiting office then I went that happened to be near,

And joined the good old Sixty-Ninth, like an Irish volunteer.

Then fill the ranks and march away! No traitors do we fear;

We'll drive them all to blazes, says the Irish volunteer!

When the Prince of Wales came over here and made a hubbaboo.

Oh, everybody turned out, you know, in gold and tinsel too;

But then the good old Sixty-Ninth didn't like these lords or peers.

They wouldn't give a damn for kings, the Irish volunteers!

We love the land of Liberty, it's the laws we will revere,

"But the devil take nobility!" says the Irish volunteer!

Now if the traitors in the South should ever cross our roads,

We'll drive them to the devil as Saint Patrick did the toads;

We'll give them all short nooses that come just below the ears,

Made strong and good of Irish hemp by Irish volunteers.

Then here's to brave McClellan, whom the army now reveres...

He'll lead us on to victory, the Irish volunteers.

Now fill your glasses up, my boys, a toast come drink with me,

May Erin's Harp and the Starry Flag united ever be;

May traitors quake and rebels shake and tremble in their fears,

When next they meet the Yankee boys and Irish volunteers!

God bless the name of Washington! That name this land reveres;

Success to Meagher and Nugent, and their Irish volunteers!

"With respect to the Kennedy assassinations, the song reflects a sobering motivation," Eli commented after he had listened.

Donna stepped out of the surf and opted for log behind his right side. "Yes, especially after McClellan's betrayal. One month before the JFK assassination, the senator received testimony from someone working for the godfather," she replied, lightening her steps as she began balancing on the surrounding logs.

"JFK's last speech in Fort Worth discussed the TFX missile," Eli observed. "During the Civil War, the Union questioned a General McClellan, a suspect in the Lincoln assassination."

"Yes, and two days prior to the assassination in Dallas, the New York Times printed that LBJ was being investigated for the TFX contract, which appeared to be favoritism."

"And the owners of the company that made the TFX represented the same bootleggers that the *Untouchables* pursued during prohibition," Eli mused, scratching his head.

"Yes, and who were owned by thinly-veiled Roman Empire, though others might say illumined ones. Get the picture? It is a familiar story. JFK's grandfather owned many saloons in the Boston area as well as a whiskey import business. He helped start the only Irish bank in Boston with his earnings. Prohibition shut him down. Bootlegging fell on the shoulders of his son. There's a difference between an Irish immigrant saving his business and a gangster associated with the Roman Empire. The US government never offered support for the transitions, like they do now."

"The robber barons ran Prohibition through Congress almost as fast as the Federal Reserve Act," Eli commented. "The sinking of the Titanic killed the Congresspeople who would have voted against the Federal Reserve during the holidays. Eliot Ness of the *Untouchables* did eventually go to work for Diebold, a company that rose with the Civil War." He rose from his position and stared at the horizon. With a sigh, he recalled Diebold's next plans to get into the electronic money and voting machine businesses. Eli stared briefly at the sand between his toes. A light breeze blew off the surf and he raised his head. In his courtroom voice, he told her, "Ness could only go so far in his prosecutions. The Canadian border restricted him. Even some of the underworld in this country would have gone against their suppliers, given those ultimate conditions. Some supported the rival bootleggers. So what tipped the scales against JFK as he confronted the pirated military-industrial-complex in a Mexican standoff?"

Donna replied, "If JFK had stepped out of the limo to shake hands with the people standing on the steps of the depository building, then half of the motorcade would have been slaughtered. Tanks would have rolled in from Fort Sam to officially claim the United States."

"Oh, I think I get it now."

"JFK had not foreseen the betrayal of his distant cousins associated with the bootlegging days. It tipped the scales against him. He did not know they had a gun on him in Fort Worth during his speech. Regardless whether the corporate machine listened, others did hear him."

"OK, so who do we have on our side?"

"We have celestials like those who travel through time to help out." Donna skipped a few stones across the waves as she spoke. Taking a breath of fresh air, she remarked, "It takes a certain amount of spiritual integrity to be a time traveler, though some just seem to provide minor comic relief and their humor can be irritating under dire circumstances. You must learn to make the most of things. Recognize the aberration in time as an opportunity to restore balance and light, maybe even move forward." Warming her hands inside her pockets, she watched the tide roll in. For a moment, she paused in deep reflection. Then she added, "My Welsh grandfather gave me a book about a time traveler once. Called *Stranger At Killknock*, the author wrote a similar book known as *The Mouse that Roared*. The movie starred Peter Sellers."

"Hmm, I never made the connection," Eli admitted. He ruefully glanced at the distant horizon.

Donna shrugged. "I learned never to underestimate the power of smallness in physics." With a grin, she took one hand out of her pocket. Waving at an overhead cloud, she reminded him, "You already have met the Thunder People."

Dusk appeared on the cape and enveloped Donna and Eli in its hue. Within a half hour, darkness would obliterate the path to the street from the beach.

"Let's leave before it the tide comes in," Eli proposed. "I don't want to rely on a time traveler to get out of this one."

"Yeah, I know. They only show in true emergencies," Donna suggested. "If you start seeing them, then you know that you are in trouble."

"Hey how about we catch the evening ferry and cruise to the Vineyard and back?" he offered. "We'll go roundtrip and catch a fish sandwich at the deli."

Laughing and stumbling over the small dunes before ascending the bluff to the street, Eli and Donna made their way to the Carmen Ghia parked on the street. At the top of the bluff, they turned and faced the night settling over the cape. The swirling, ebony air haunted them. They hopped in the car, looking forward to a change of scenery.

The couple left the Carmen Ghia parked at the dock and bought refreshments before boarding. Then they went to the upper deck where they began munching on their sandwiches in the soft sea breeze. Standing over the rails while peering out to sea, Donna began, "My friend Eric, the paleontologist, came to this planet as a pilgrim in a past life."

"Why am I not surprised? I knew there was a deeper meaning to the Plymouth tale," Eli reasoned as he leaned back against the outside cabin wall and smiled confidently. Spreading his arms wide and opening his palms, he seemed ready for any story now, though he wanted to humor himself first. "Your words are more than just a wandering metaphor, especially with Sparky around," he stated. He looked at the skies after coining his own affectionate-term for the Thunder People. Then he lowered his head and met her gaze.

Donna chuckled. She quickly turned and faced Eli. "Look, I don't make the rules on this planet. I just happen to live here."

"I suppose that your sidekick in the paleontology department studies Sparky with his other scientifically repressed colleagues," he lightly teased her.

"How did you know?" Donna questioned, turning around to ignore any ensuing sarcasm.

Leaving his position against the wall, Eli laughed as he wrapped his arms around her. He smiled, smelling the herbal scent in her hair. Donna laughed too. She enjoyed his gentle snuggle in the cooling sea air.

Chapter Fifteen

If you manage to avoid
America's suicide-machine
You must fight against
Being labeled a 'tramp'

Tune Reference: *Born to Run*
----Bruce Springsteen

WHEN THE FERRY stopped at the dock at the other end of the cape, Eli watched the passengers unload. Donna stepped away from him and scouted the black horizon under the dimness of the crescent moon. Late in the evening, only a small group of people came onboard, while the ship seemed to wait for eternity in the quiet waters. Finally, the ferry embarked for the final round.

Halfway across the cape, Eli began talking softly in her nondominant left ear. "I have some changes to make," he told her. "Don't go looking for me. I will contact you when I reach safety."

"Was it something I said?" Donna said lightly with a serious tone and toss of her head. "I figured you'd join Runner's Anonymous, once you heard it from a card-carrying member."

She nestled her face in his chest as he held her gently. Pausing briefly, she confessed, "I felt called by the surf this afternoon. I didn't expect to find you there. I almost ran. I like to think that I have difficulty falling in love and seeing it through, but it really isn't true. It easier to fight a thousand enemies than find love on the run."

Eli squeezed her tenderly as he held her. "I called you at the surf. I wanted to see you again." His tone matched her seriousness. After a slight pause, he suggested, "Let's get off the boat separately. We are dealing with dangerous people who kill in altered states. The *nadas* have intergalactic connections that we cannot ignore. When I start seeing white lights in the sky, it is time to go. I just saw someone who I recognize from the investigation. He doesn't see me, but I did not expect him to depart from the Vineyard at this hour. It resonates with what you have told me today. I'll get McClendon to give me a ride back. I'll leave the Carmen Ghia as a decoy, so they think I went for an overnight on the Vineyard. It will give me a head start." Then he released her. "I love you," he told her as he gently guided her towards the other end of the ferry in the darkness.

Donna subtly squeezed the ring finger of his right hand in acknowledgement, before surrendering into the current of his forceful words. She let it carry her to the stairwell without a moment's hesitation. Descending the stairs into the lighted lobby, she veered away from the people collected in the dining area. Donna ducked into the woman's restroom and hid there until the ferry dock began unloading. Taking care to leave the ferry in the shadows, she lumbered behind the people leaving the ferry. Donna chose a direction opposite the crowd and found her way back to the studio apartment.

After saying good-bye, Eli watched Donna make her way down the stairs. When she disappeared out of his view, he sought refuge under the shadows of the cabin wall. There, he waited until he saw the people on the ferry twenty yards ahead on the dock. Then he swiftly left his post. He stopped to determine the location of the people ahead of him and noticed that they had paused to marvel at the Carmen Ghia. Someone recognized his car. They laughed and hurried up the street where a blue sedan picked them up. He watched the car drive away and tracked the movement of the headlights on the highway overlooking the bluff. Eli raced to the Blue Heron where he telephoned Dr. McClendon for a ride back to Boston.

At the apartment, Donna stood in the middle of the room and contemplated her next move. She started packing her things for an emergency flight. After a cup of rosemary tea, Donna went to bed and rested. Early the next morning, she heard a knock at the door. Looking through the peephole on the door, Donna recognized the face of her training brother from class. She threw on a sweatshirt while the young man on the other side of the door talked to her. He didn't waste anytime waiting for her to dress.

"Dr. McClendon wants to meet you at the lab," he said. Then he left, confidant that Donna had heard him.

She exited the apartment moments behind him and quickly walked towards the geophysics building. As a result of training together, the class learned to detect each other's every movement making words unnecessary. They understood without sentiment. She opened the door to the office and found Dr. McClendon sitting on one of the computer desks, like an officer explaining a military mission.

"If anyone asks where you were last night, tell them that you were here with me working overtime on the seismic data. Eli found that they had already trashed his office last night. Must be getting desperate and bolder. Somebody rummaged his files, which fortunately were kept elsewhere. As far as you know, he went sailing alone yesterday afternoon. The Coast Guard is looking for him."

Donna appreciated the briefing. She watched Dr. McClendon leave his perch on the computer desk. He retrieved a letter from his shirt pocket and handed it to Donna.

The note read: Dear Donna, I disappeared. Love, Eli.

"Simple, sweet, and to the point," Donna remarked, shaking her head at the complicated turn of events. Succinct, almost to the point of irritation, the lawyer proved to be a man of few words. "OK, now what?"

"We wait and keep training," Dr. McClendon assured her. "See you at class."

Donna left. She journeyed to the outskirts of town to visit Eric. He shared an apartment with his roommate Bob, who answered the door when she knocked.

"Oh you must be Eric's buddy, Donna," Bob greeted, extending a handshake. He had been out late working in the paleontology lab and appeared bedraggled this Saturday morning. "Eric went to the airport to pick up his girlfriend. I think they had plans to go to Nantucket Beach this afternoon. I'll let him know you came by."

Donna laughed when she remembered how Terri restored order in Eric's life like no one else. Waving Bob back into his lair, she went back to her apartment to regroup for class. By the next day, the local papers ran the following headlines: "Boston Lawyer Lost at Sea" and "Coast Guard Looking for Missing Attorney."

Initially, she could shrug off the news, but by the end of the weekend she felt overwhelmed. After avoiding the newsstands, she sauntered into class after Friday's lunch. Joan and several of Donna's training brothers stretched on the mat. Dr. McClendon smiled and bowed in the traditional greeting as if nothing seemed askew in their world. In a quiet voice, he told her, "Joan has some knowledge that can help you. She knows what has happened. Talk to her in the treatment room after class."

Joan acknowledged Dr. McClendon's introduction with a silent nod at Donna. Together they joined their classmates and resumed stretching on the floor. Donna relaxed and found comfort in the cheerful faces surrounding her. No longer isolated in an individual's experience, each entertained a different perspective.

After practice she met Joan down the hallway leading to the treatment room. The room contained a massage table, a few soft chairs, and an assortment of medicinal vials and jars of botanicals. Joan pulled open a drawer of homeopathic vials from a traditional medicine chest sitting on a small oak desk. She smiled as she sat in the chair facing the chest while musing, "Even though homeopathy is really a German invention, we use it here in the training hall because it fits the intention of the place."

Joan retrieved a vial from the assortment and poured some of the contents into a small dispensary cup. "Not only do you need to make your energy invisible to the perpetrators, but you will need a clear head and intact physiology. Here, I suggest this remedy named after a fascist saint."

After handing the small cup to Donna, Joan leaned back while commenting further, "It is for hysteria, especially in the strong silent types. The only way one would notice anything amiss is by the proverbial lump in their throats. It also provides protection from secret societies and inquisitions."

"I could use that protection now. I may be heading into an inquisition for all I know," she replied with slight chagrin. Accepting the cup, Donna ingested the contents of the cup sublingually. She raised her eyebrows when the energy of the remedy resonated within her entire being.

Joan sensed the immediate shift in Donna's electromagnetic field and felt relieved that she had found the correct remedy. "A single dose of Ignatia initiates changes in the body for nine days. Coffee tends to antidote homeopathics, so avoid this for a week."

"No worries there. I never developed a taste for coffee. Too much to wake up to in the morning as it is," Donna answered.

"Call me if you ever need my help," Joan instructed. "Dr. McClendon knows how to contact me."

"Thank you," Donna said, rising from her chair. "I'm ready for a long overdue nap."

Joan noticed her sleepiness and grinned. With years of experience in tracking homeopathic case, she enjoyed noting the subtle signs of rejuvenation. No longer in imminent danger, Donna required rest.

After Donna exited the training hall, Dr. McClendon came out of the reception area and lightly rubbed Joan's back. "How is she?" he inquired.

"Exhausted, but she responded well to the homeopathic. There is so much more to be done. We may be gaining her trust."

Joan turned and faced Dr. McClendon, who began drawing her in a long sensuous kiss. She returned his embrace, fervently rubbing his ears and head as she joined his lips. They paused for a brief interlude as he turned off the lights and secured the front door. Together they headed back towards the low lights of the treatment room and locked the door.

Returning to her apartment, Donna snacked and went to sleep for the night. The next day Donna awoke refreshed. Grateful for Joan's intervention, Donna stretched in the morning light of a new dawn, one offering new possibilities and giving her a chance in life. She enjoyed breakfast and then showered. Reentering the living area, she noticed that someone had taped a red envelope to the sliding glass door on the balcony. When Donna recognized the red envelope with the Green Dragon logo on it, she chuckled. She reasoned that one of her classmates lived close to her in the same apartment complex, or had a friend that did.

Opening the letter, she read another cryptic note from Eli: Meet me at the Blue Heron at eight o'clock tonight.

Tossing the letter aside on the breakfast bar, Donna paced the room for a moment. Then she busied herself with light errands. In contrast to Eli's peripheral presence, she seemed like an agent on the inside trying to come out. Looking out the window, she watched two ships pass by each other. The gray hull glistened like silver in the daylight, flickering in the other's reflections with flags swaying above them. They appeared ready to meet at the next port, despite coming from opposite directions.

After running down her options, Donna felt her heart race as she swung open the familiar blue doors leading inside the restaurant. A touch of chagrin tugged at the corners of her mouth as she became aware of his effect on her heart. She peered into the dining area and looked for Eli. He sat at the same table where they had met earlier. Seeing her at the door, he rose from the table to warmly hug her.

Donna fell into his embrace, seeming to merge with his being without any restraint. It lasted only a second before they sat down and ordered glasses of Merlot.

"You're a sight for sore eyes," she told him while determining her order from the menu she opened in front of him. Somewhere in the irrational depths of her heart, she felt annoyed by his sudden disappearance.

He teased her back. "You're one to talk."

Donna hung her head slightly and looked up at him with wide eyes, reminiscent of a netted tiger. Caught in the circumstances, Donna leaned back in her chair and sighed. Their brief greeting served as the first time anyone had thrown her own scene in her face. Staring at his soft blue eyes and unshaven face, she found herself in the reflection. Something inside her yelled "Ouch." She sipped the red wine brought by the waitress. With his watchcap and wool jacket, he looked more like an area fisherman rather than an attorney. She admired his easy diversity and smiled.

"So what are you going to do now?" Donna asked after the waitress brought their plates of food.

Eli reached for her right hand across the table and gazed into her eyes. "Finish up loose ends. Keep blowing smoke in their faces, and get to know you better."

Donna stared at his hands for a moment and agreed, "Any more details?"

"A few, but mostly work-related. It is amazing how much I can do behind the scenes and still make a living. I may reappear or I may not reappear. I have a whole new perspective on life that I want explore. I leave tonight for a three-day trip and I want to stay in contact with you. I love you."

Donna withdrew from his touch, thoughtfully brought both hands to her lips in a relaxed prayer pose. She slightly bent her head over crossed index fingers. "I love you," she said in the manner of the thinker reflecting on a boulder.

Eli leaned back and smiled. His eyes glistened as he savored all the new possibilities tumbling into his life. Reaching across the table, he grasped both of her hands in his. He looked into Donna's eyes while he spoke, "I will contact you while I am gone through Dr. McClendon. It will keep the focus off of you. I want you to be careful."

Then he lessened his grasp and softly kissed her hands. Donna slightly blushed. He resumed his position across the table as quick as he had left it. Nobody in the restaurant had been aware of their brief but intimate interlude. The couple did not overplay their luck. Instead they smiled sweetly at each other and began eating. Afterwards they left the table separately to avoid publicizing the fact that they were a couple. Donna walked back to her apartment under the shadows checkering the dimly lit streets. Eli left a few moments later and headed in the opposite direction into the darkness.

Chapter Sixteen

You can find redemption

In a streetlight

If you have hope

Tune Reference: *Don't Stop Believing*

----Journey

WITH A GRIMACE, Eli reluctantly departed from Donna. Bowing his head with hands clasped tightly behind his back, he paced the streets. He resolutely walked towards an old light green Chevy truck around the corner, and jumped in the driver's seat. After settling in the comfort of this reliable hunk of machinery, he started the motor and vowed that he would never be forced to leave her in the future. Determined to see her again, he grimaced as his heart ached, while veering the truck onto the highway for Boston. Their lives had been intensely thrown together in a crucible during the past week, creating alchemy between them that he could not ignore. Regardless whether Donna understood, he did. Their spiritual destinies had somehow melded together. This awareness helped him find his way in the night towards Boston. His shoulders relaxed as he blinked at the greenish-white lights on the vehicle's control panel.

Eli drove to a group of old gray warehouses on the industrialized bay. Though much of the city's population had abandoned the area years ago, he owned a flat conveniently adjacent to the intellectual hub of the world. He had many reliable contacts in the vicinity. Despite its shabby outside appearance, the flat consisted of two modern, comfortable apartments that afforded a view of MIT and Harvard from across the Charles River. Removed from the mindless realm of gossip and slander, the inhabitants either put their nose in a book or quickly passed through.

After parking the truck in the underground garage, he climbed the stairs and unlocked the door to his familiar digs. He toured the main apartment to be sure that nothing was amiss and then slept soundly for the night. The next day he awoke to the thunder of passing cars and trucks, as morning light streaked through the tall double-framed windows and onto his pillow. Spending a few moments in the sunbeam to contemplate his next course of action, he went into the kitchen for a cup of herb tea, before beginning an exercise discipline that he had learned with Dr. McClendon many years ago. Then he sat down to breakfast and showered before leaving.

First, he paid a call on some of his associates doing research at MIT. He urged them to break connection with the company he had investigated. The mission didn't prove difficult.

"What do you mean the lead scientist committed suicide after an interview with a popular magazine yesterday afternoon?" he questioned his colleagues, who were still apparently in shock.

"I don't get it," they replied almost in unison. "He had everything going for him."

"How about 'suicided'?" Eli asked.

"They found the gun in his right," one scientist stated, before pausing to reflect. He added in a daze, "But I always thought he was left handed."

"Alright, I get it," Eli admitted, exiting the room as quickly as he had entered. Without further explanation, he told them, "If anyone comes looking for me, tell them that I am missing."

"Got it," the group waved at him. "Some of us are on extended vacations and sabbaticals."

"Good idea," Eli reminded them before leaving, "This conversation didn't happen."

Past lunchtime, Eli completed his errands on the university campus. He decided to visit a popular Irish pub known as the Green Dragon Tavern. Although the original tavern had been demolished shortly before the Civil War, the north-end model possessed the mystique from the one built in the 1600's. Known as the Green Dragon Tavern long before occultists bought it for meetings, the company patriots renamed it 'Saint Andrews Lodge.' The locals still referred to the tavern as the Green Dragon, which once boasted the largest room for meetings in northern Boston during the American Revolution. The inspiration for the Paul Revere's ride and Boston Tea Party literally came from the spirits poured at the Green Dragon Tavern.

Eli ordered a stout along with a plate of fish and salad. The waitress brought the stout immediately and he began savoring the thick dark beer. Noting his placid surroundings, he allowed the revelations of the morning to drip over him like rain. He recalled other cases where the key players suddenly disappeared and he thought about his next courses of action.

Pulling out schedule book from his knapsack, he checked tomorrow's plans to go to the Environmental Protection Agency (EPA) with his findings. He considered his colleague in EPA as an honest man, who would not betray his whereabouts. Eli underlined his notes on transferring the investigation to the government. If they cited the factory as a hazardous waste site, the doors would close and the covert manufacturing of bombs would stop. He perused his options and considered alternatives. The brainwashed witnesses would have difficulty recovering. After all the intrigue, it would take some time for them to figure out their own story. Glancing at his watch, he decided to cut his losses and investigate other cases.

His thoughts strayed to Donna, who had somehow managed to survive and escape mind-control games. She had not sold out yet and never would. Donna made it all look easy with her Thunder People, time travelers, and hippie scientists.

He counted all the people supported his efforts. They may not be violent, deranged, or corrupt, but they remained powerful in their own right. He would have to learn how to talk to this majority to get his point across. It would take time, but this seemed the key to his new beginning.

The waitress placed the rest of his order on the table and he started eating. He wondered what this international group would do next and what they wanted. Why did the workings of a small factory matter to them? Why snuff out a scientist or a lawyer? Were such individuals really such a threat? Why did they just hit without bothering to run or hide? What did they have to lose? Even if their motives were discovered, what could be done about it? What should be done?

Eli finished and paid for his lunch. Walking outside of the Green Dragon Tavern seemed like heading back into the night. The light of those who had gone before him rested with the spirit of the Green Dragon. Some of the light seemed only to illuminate, while others possessed a true light. He passed a few newspaper stands and read the headlines. One headline particularly intrigued him and he bought a paper from a time traveler. Casually wearing attire from the early 1900's, the man hawked the papers near the stand. He had an old-fashioned business air about him. His clear amber eyes singled Eli out of the crowd, drawing him in personally.

"Thanks, mate," he replied when Eli handed him some silver coins in exchange for the paper. "Read all about it," he said with a wink, before resuming his business. No one else on the street seemed to notice the anomaly except Eli. People rushed by or nonchalantly bought a paper without making eye contact.

Glancing at the article, Eli understood why he needed the newspaper. He straightened as a shudder ran up his spine. Apparently, someone had hot-wired the Carmen Ghia and taken it for a cruise down the highway towards Plymouth. The Coast Guard had fished it from the bottom of the cape near where it had missed a turn. They matched the body to the lawyer who own the car. Eli looked at the picture of the man who had been found in the car. He recognized the face of the man who he had avoided on the ferry.

Eli folded the paper and headed for the federal depository library, another favorite haunt where he felt safe. Security guards lined many rows of tall thick bookshelves and procured spaces for hiding. If his pursuers inquired at the front desk, the staff would evade their approach. Intent on reading, they cared even less about intrigue and smugly hid from the world themselves. Besides, he professed no intention of quibbling with the news; he just wanted to sit-down and finish reading the article. Walking across the mall, he decided to figure out why someone had taken his place at the bottom of the cape. Had it been a matter of snakes going after other snakes? He could not ascertain the depth of his investigation. This library held plenty of volumes on cases for needed references. He wondered about the legal ramifications of somebody claiming to be his body and what to do when the claimant is deceased.

The time traveler at the newsstand had literally handed him a legal handle on the case. What a great way to blow smoke in their faces---like a Green dragon! Puff! Puff! What illusions he could create to thwart their operations from a safe vantage point!

Donna loomed in his thoughts. She seemed to make this complicated world so simple. He wished to turn this sordid tale around to his advantage, so that he could easily spend the rest of his life with her. Aside from the intrigues of his life, a greater mystery beckoned him.

Chapter Seventeen

Celestial dreams of numbers

Sometimes 25 or 6 to 4

Sometimes 666, sometimes 555

Sometimes 888

When the math doesn't add up

Remember that it is only a number

Tune Reference: *25 or 6 to 4*

----Chicago

THE NEXT DAY Eli took his information to the EPA office. A wide-eyed secretary informed the office manager that Eli had arrived for his prescheduled appointment. The office manager immediately came out and greeted Eli. He hurriedly ushered Eli into his office.

"I saw the headlines," Harry began. "Although the photo did not look like you, I wondered whether you were to going to show up today. I am glad you did. It appears that the lead scientist really is dead. Whatever happened must have hit a nerve."

"All I did was avoid showing up for work. The office had already been trashed. What did they expect me to do? The photograph of the man in the paper is one of the managers of the company I investigated. When I saw him follow me on the last Vineyard ferry, I decided to leave my car on the dock. The company attempted to kill the geophysicist who produced this data."

Taking a deep breath, Eli eyed Harry. He confided, "I suspected that they might come after me and left my car on the dock. I watched the man and his group checking out the Carmen Ghia. They hot-wired the vehicle and he drove away in my car. They did not see me. The reporters fabricated the rest."

"You know that this is no longer just a hazardous waste problem," Harry remarked as he picked up the pile of papers.

"Yes, but the first step is to have it declared as one." Eli produced a copy of another newspaper headline that he had found at the library: *Childhood Leukemia Epidemic in Framingham.* "Here, there are numerous hazardous sites near this area. It's something else that they want hushed."

He handed it to Harry as he produced a map showing the vicinity of the company to this location. "Unlike JFK, it is not too late for us to get out of the crossfire."

Harry hummed to himself, while looking over the documents. "Has the company started calling you 'Silkwood' yet?" 'Silkwood' referred to the name of a whistleblower investigating high levels of plutonium at the Kerr-McGee plant in Oklahoma. She died under mysterious circumstances, while driving to deliver documents to a New York Times reporter. Afterwards, Twentieth-Century Fox made a movie about the incident.

"The geophysicist mentioned that the crew from the company referred to her as 'Silkwood,'" Eli answered. "I'm not talking to reporters. They are murderers."

"That's always a good policy these days," Harry agreed, before setting the papers down and looking at Eli.

"I am turning the case over to a firm that will prosecute," Eli announced. Then he added, anticipating Harry's reaction, "Your job is safe and easy."

"Thanks, Eli," Harry replied. "I like to go home at the end of the day and see my family."

"I'd like to have a family," Eli admitted.

Harry eyed Eli and chuckled. "A fresh young defender of justice like you?"

"Actually, I'm interested in the geophysicist that they called 'Silkwood,'" Eli admitted.

"OK, let's look at what we are up against before biting off more than we can chew," Harry began. "Do you think the underworld is involved?"

"This is Boston," Eli replied. "They fought over water long before Prohibition."

"Prohibition is just another word for British invasion."

"Said like a true Eagle."

"Most of the liquor illegally imported into this country came from one Canadian company," Harry continued. "The Canadians readied themselves for Prohibition."

"British Empire," Eli piped. "The empire had British Intelligence operatives as well as the underworld running their stuff. Did the monarchy come first or was it the East India Company?"

"This time they ran alcohol instead of opium, tea, and slaves. Same corporate monarchy but different employees."

"Now can you recall the name of the company targeted in the Boston Tea Party?" Eli quizzed. "Remember that they dumped opium as well as tea. In the early 1900's, the United States made opium illegal."

"The East India company ran the district, the one they call Washington D.C.." Harry swiveled around in his chair and sighed. "The same ones associated with the opium wars in China. China prohibited opium during the American Revolution, and history showed that it increased the use. The effect of prohibiting opium in Asia proved essentially equivalent to prohibiting alcohol in the West. The ancient Asian cultures used opium in religious rituals, whereas alcohol is more traditional in western civilizations. Westerners associate liquor with community as well as sacred rites of passage. Even George Washington made his own beer."

"Now think about the timing of Prohibition," Eli urged. "Many soldiers that had a drink during WWI would have obtained that alcohol illegally through British Intelligence or underworld operatives. Can you see some unhealthy relationships developing under this scenario?"

"Like the military-industrial complex," Eli observed. "Or Watergate."

"Now the origins of the United States differed from most colonies. The terrain included a melting pot of immigrants and natives," Harry explained, leaning back in his chair. "Most immigrants came to this country to avoid genocide either directly or indirectly through economic terrorism. The corporate monarchies are the last thing that an immigrant wants to see." Moving closer toward Eli, he waved an arm in the air as if he wished to dismiss the topic. "The underworld that invades the turf is already employed by the monarchists, science cabal, orthodox religious, Zionists, and Vatican. The underworld doesn't buy into independence because they are codependent. Life, liberty, or the pursuit of happiness is meaningless to them."

Eli persisted, "Three years ago I won a case against this company for exposing their employees to benzene. Now I am finding evidence of mind control in making illegal nuclear plastics. The commodity in question here is radiation."

Harry reflected, "I've seen a few cases like this reach the Department of Justice. They do not go very far. Nuclear blackmail involves a variety of international gangs."

"So somebody already got to them?" Eli questioned.

"Apparently some of the devices are already in significant places," Harry determined.

"It is a perpetual Cuban Missile Crisis," Eli observed.

"The good news is that nuclear power plants aren't as popular," Harry happily said. "One source of nuclear blackmail might go out of existence."

"We are still here, even after the *coup d'etat* of the JFK assassination, which I am only beginning to understand," Eli stated ruefully.

"You and your love interest are still here," Harry reminded. "Anything or anyone could change the balance."

"I appreciate your wisdom," Eli acknowledged.

Harry grinned and rose to shake Eli's hand. "Enough said. I'll do my part. Get out of here. Just send me a wedding invitation."

Eli brightened and met his handshake. He waved at the wide-eyed receptionist as he walked out. Outside the building, a bright sun warmed him from across the extensive brick. His truck remained on the street, parked where he had left it. After his conversation at the EPA, there remained only one place where he wanted to go. He sped out of the city and took the highway to Marblehead, a rugged fishing town off the Massachusetts coast.

The dark rocky beaches of Marblehead attracted him. Its streets and harbor spoke of the shipping commerce of days gone by. A multitude of colored sea glass from the refuse of many vessels washed on the shore and shone on the dark sand like exotic shiny jewels. Eli relished picking up and examining the glass bits, wondering the origin of each piece and the tales the fragment could tell. After parking his truck along the beachfront, he bought a crab roll and sat on one of the crags extending towards the water. He listened quietly to the small waves as the tide came in. A seagull flew in to help him with his lunch. Eli waved him away and the gull complied.

He watched the neat lineup of yachts in the distant harbor. As the shipping industry had faded with history, the city emerged as the 'yachting capital of the world.' Not many sailors took advantage of the relatively calm weather today. All the movement on the beach seemed to be holding its breath, waiting for an explosion of action, perhaps to resurface from the past. Eli rose and skipped a few rocks across the calm waters. The words of his friend reciting his father's favorite phrase came to mind: "When dawn breaks on Marblehead..."

Somehow that phrase held significance for a commercial airline pilot, who relied on modern equipment for navigation and timing. This small town greeted the sunrise before most people on the busy east coast. *What did it mean?* He imagined that dawn breaking on Marblehead would be spectacular.

His friend died, possibly the victim of foul play. With his partner, he created a wonderful high-tech venture that fostered goodwill in the world. The details of the enterprise or the plane crash never interested him. Freedom from the syntax, gave him the chance to mourn and recall the echoes of his companion with a simple phrase, "When dawn breaks on Marblehead..."

Feeling the icy, hardness of an internalized dagger thaw inside him, Eli climbed on one of the rocky ledges. Groups of gulls and crows hovered around him as he released the attack on his friend. Looking around from the minor height of the rocks, he remembered that his ancestors had been artisans from Germany in the 1800's. They came to this continent because they wanted a freer place to pursue better products. This sense for personal and artistic refinement matched the spectacular when-dawn-breaks-on-Marblehead phrase. This he could understand. They had not suffered. He had not suffered. He descended from a lineage of insufferable artists, intent on the joy of living. Sometimes the biggest thrill came with being able to wake-up and see the dawn.

Sensing the dawning of his soul, he astutely studied his surroundings. There, in the middle of this sleepy little coastal town, he realized that he could make things happen. He needed to find Donna. Wishing to disrupt his downward spiral into the realm of covert affairs, Eli wanted to spend the rest of his life with her. If he, a law school graduate, could not convince the love of his life to marry him, then Eli figured that he could demand a refund for the education. Tossing off the fantasy with shrug of his shoulders, he walked back to his car and found renewed confidence for his next undertaking.

Taking the coastal highway back to Woodsport, Eli wondered where he might find her. His impatience caused him to desperately grip the steering wheel as he made a few tight turns. Arriving a day early, he considered trying the beach, one of her favorite haunts. The charm had worked the previous month, after she partnered with him on the enchantment. The two-to-three hour drive gave him plenty of time to tune in.

By the time he arrived in town, Eli changed his mind and decided to check on Donna at her apartment. After parking the truck in a nearby sandy lot, he scanned the second story of the building for signs of life at her apartment. Seeing the lights on, he sensed that he had found the right place.

He climbed the stairs to her door and looked out at her view of the cape, finally understanding the source of her inspiration.

Wishing to avoid startling her with an untimely appearance, he rapped softly on the door. Donna checked the peephole and quickly opened the door with a gasp. Overjoyed to see him, she threw her arms around Eli's neck and pulled him into the room. After kissing his cheek several times, she stood back to get a better look at him. He still had not shaved and he looked even more like an east-coast fisherman.

"I want to ask you out on a date. How about dinner at the Wayside Inn in Sudsbury?"

Donna clapped her hands together and hopped lightly delight. "Let's go!"

"Bring your things. I want to show you my digs. We can change there for dinner. I haven't much time. If I don't you bring back before work tomorrow morning, McClendon will be after us both."

Donna laughed as she grabbed a dress, heels, and a few other essentials. Within minutes, they loaded the truck and headed up the highway to Boston. Chatting away amiably during the drive, they told each other about how they had passed their time in each other's absence. Eli parked the car in the underground garage and ushered Donna up the steep stairs leading to his door. He let her in. She curiously smiled as she studied his environment like a geologist with a rock formation, lightly running her eyes over the room as if they politely touched every object like a blind person. Eli's eyes gleamed as he watched her. Then he directed her to the adjacent flat behind a locked door down the hall. "You can get ready here, an entire studio to yourself. See you in a bit. Knock on my door when you are ready."

Donna quickly made herself at home in the luxurious, one-room studio decorated in bold masculine reds and browns. She hurried in the shower and refreshed herself. Minutes later, she knocked on the door to Eli's apartment, who quickly opened the door and stepped out into the hall, locking the door behind him. He emerged handsomely dressed in a black suit with yellow oxford-dress shirt and conservative tie. Donna wore a burgundy dress with black, thin-heeled shoes. Together they made a bright, stunning couple.

An hour later, Eli opened the car door for Donna and escorted her inside the Wayside Inn. The poet Longfellow became inspired by the ambiance of the tavern and penned a series of collected works entitled *The Tales of the Wayside Inn*. Originally the inn served as a gathering place for travelers along the first mail route in the United States. The entrance to the restaurant traversed along a beautiful road lined with trees on both sides. Everything about the inn felt soft and cozy from the trees sheltering the road to the warm candlelight on the wood tables. Tall picture windows lined the dining hall, illuminating the lush landscape surrounding the diners.

"Lafayette came here, too," Donna remarked as she read a historical marker at the entrance of the dining hall.

"But, he stayed at Marblehead," Eli interjected.

The waitress seated them at a private table adjacent one of the picture windows. Donna enjoyed staring at the reflection of the dining-room candles in the dining room transposed on the glass separating them from the dusky woods.

She read the disclosure on the menu and provided a narration. "The French promised that if the British ever invaded this continent again, then they would come to the aid of the United States. Not only did they turn the tide in the American Revolution, they prevented the British from burning down the capital in the War of 1812," Donna explained. "The French intellectuals envied the American case for independence. King Louie and his Queen Marie Antoinette lost their heads for it. Their portraits adorn the rooms of Independence Hall in Philadelphia."

"It seems that the British had more to do with their overthrow rather than the peasants," Eli stated.

Putting the menu down, she glanced at the wood walls and commented, "Many parallels exist between the assassination of JFK and the attempted assassination on De Gaulle in 1962. Jackie had been a liaison between French and American Intelligence groups after WWII, when De Gaulle eventually reassumed a leadership role in France. He had organized the French resistance in WWII." Donna paused for a moment, before sipping a glass of red wine. "A former liaison sat next to her on Air Force One near the casket. The Secret Service seized the body from the hospital at gunpoint. Colonel Prouty wrote that the liaison and JFK had been competitors, but I doubt it pertained to romantic interests. I suspect that the competition pertained to opposing national interests."

Their salad arrived and Eli passed the butter over to Donna for her bread. She buttered her bread over her salad while adding, "The Kennedys maintained a relationship with French Intelligence. Unlike a French connection or farewell America, which ironically are titles of books that came out around the time of the RFK assassination, the relationship cultivated more respect and positivity. De Gaulle considered Jackie the most knowledgeable woman on the French." Putting her buttered bread down on a plate, she lowered her eyes and said succinctly, "I suggest you pursue these associations."

Eli quickly finished his salad, then sat back and fingered his glass of red wine as he listened to the young woman across from him. He watched her thoughtfully linger over her salad, carefully choosing her portions so that she didn't bite off more than she could chew. After a momentary silence, she glanced at Eli and realized that he closely watched her in fascination. The motions of the waiter and waitress distracted her from her discomfort. They simultaneously appeared and removed the salad bowl, while replacing the dishes with the main course. Eli abruptly ended his stare and dove into his Shepherd's Pie. Meanwhile, Donna intently focused on eating her Seafood Normandy.

Finishing her meal, she looked up and noticed Eli observing her. Donna pushed her plate to the side for the waitress to pick up, before reaching across and lightly touching Eli's hands. He brightened with her touch, eagerly waiting to hear what else she would say.

Donna did not disappoint. "I suggest taking your case to the Kennedy's French relations. Do your research and invoke the French-American Alliance from the American Revolution. It may take you over ten years, but in time, the pieces of the puzzle will come together and reveal the truth. If they don't, then we know the extent of the betrayal."

Withdrawing her hand, she leaned back in her chair. Thoughtfully, she observed the reflections of the candles in the glass windows as she finished the last sip of her wine. Their satisfying experience left no room for desert in the intense course of the evening. She waved the waitress off, while Eli asked for the check.

When the waitress had left the scene, Eli looked directly at her. "Got it," he said rather seriously as if he had been given a briefing.

Together they left the Wayside Inn and waited for the valet to retrieve the truck. Instead of driving through Boston, Eli drove the back roads to the cape. Listening to music under the soft glow of the truck's instrument panel, their conversation grew light. As promised, Eli returned Donna to her apartment at a reasonable hour, so she could rest for work the next morning. He helped her climb down from the truck and escorted her up the stairs leading to her studio. After Donna unlocked the front door, he dashed inside the front room to avoid being seen. She turned and locked the door behind them.

He reached for her and she responded to his embrace. She closed her eyes as his soft moist lips found her, yielding to another world. Cradling his face in her hands she drunk in the fullness of his soul and being. For a moment they melded into the other and found another dimension, another plane of existence where they transcended time and space, a place where nothing else could touch them. They went beyond themselves. Eli touched and filled her. He longed to stay with her essence forever and traversed this new, unfamiliar terrain that somehow knew him better than himself. Swimming together in this vortex as waves of emotion and passion came crashing down on them, they conducted the impact through their bodies and felt refreshed with the vibration resonating through their enmeshed souls. He drew back his kiss, only to plunge further into the depths bringing her with him in a breathless dive. Donna lost herself in his fervent warmth and then found him standing before her in a void, where she experienced a radiance so encompassing that it overwhelmed all her senses.

A sudden knock on the door slowed them down. Donna pulled herself from Eli and looked through the peephole. "It's Eric," she said. "He knows I'm here. I can tell by the determined look on his face."

Meanwhile, Eli had already slipped out the sliding glass door to the back balcony. He gave her a smiling salute and waved her off. Then he resolutely turned his back on her and leaped over the rail like a swift ninja.

Deciding that she would figure out the route that her friends used to get to and from her balcony tomorrow, she quietly opened the door.

Eric bounced in the room. "Wow, you look nice! What rock formations have you been studying lately?"

"Quiet," Donna told him before changing the subject.

Eric dropped his arms to his side. With a mild sighed, he provided a hint of resignation. He paced the floor for a few steps and looked out of the corner of his eye. Donna met his stare, but never answered his question. He sighed, realizing that would never get his desired response. She questioned, "What's going on? Where's your girlfriend?"

"Oh, Terri wanted to get to bed early for tonight, because she has work tomorrow," he replied.

"I see," Donna said with a nod. "Sounds like a great idea to me."

The clock on the wall read ten o'clock. She sat down on the small couch, and took off her high heels. Rubbing her head as if to wake up from a long dream, she realized that she had not regained her composure after Eli's kiss.

"McClendon wanted me to let you know that all the computers are down in the science buildings."

"Isn't that odd?"

"We think so, too," Eric confirmed. "We thought that you should know. Both McClendon and I consider it is a warning to stay alert."

"Thanks," Donna responded. "I need to get to bed. Looks like there will be a lot of work to do tomorrow."

Eric grinned, anticipating the mayhem of the morning. "You're right. I'll catch you later."

Then he warmly smiled and exited the room after a slight bow. Donna laughed and threw a small pillow at him before he left. Eric jumped to dodge the pillow. He laughed as he ran out the door, which Donna immediately locked behind him. Then she closed the drapes around the sliding glass door, and headed to the kitchenette to brew a cup of chamomile tea.

Chapter Eighteen

To be saved from love

Never underestimate

The truth of its

Aphrodisiac quality

Tune Reference: *Addicted to Love*

----Robert Palmer

THE NEXT DAY Donna awoke and hurried to the geophysics office. She found Dr. McClendon standing near the computer, restoring backup data. He appeared calm and smiled at her when she walked in. "Hi," he greeted. "The computers are running now. You did a great job of maintaining backups. It's going easy."

Donna nodded and checked on her data. Given the circumstances, the office expected a computer glitch to threaten their work. Regardless whether the problem stemmed from adversity or inertia, she took no chances with moving forward. She focused on her task and minimized risk. Dr. McClendon noticed her silence and kept his distance with a watchful eye. Seeing the panic in her eyes, he sensed Donna's loss for words. Her relationship with those in her class seemed more intuitive, probably because they trained together regularly now.

Leaving work in the early evening, she stepped outside in the glare of the setting sun mirrored in little ripples on the cape. Filling her lungs with the changing sea breeze, her thoughts lingered with the mists settling over the beach where she had seen the hummingbird. Donna turned away from her studio and ventured toward the familiar log. She wondered whether she would meet Eli there again. On the bluff ahead, some men in dress suits overlooked the beach with binoculars. Compared to the vacant beach and calm gray waters, they appeared mean and rough. Donna noticed that if she continued on the path down the bluff, they would spot her. Turning around, she returned to her apartment.

At the top of the stairs, she stopped and gazed at the sea. The men on the bluff scoured the area with their scopes. She hurriedly unlocked the door and went in. Somebody had taped another red envelope on the sliding glass door. Donna retrieved it, before sitting down on the couch to read it. Wishing to maintain her low profile, she had not bothered to install a telephone.

The letter came from Eli. He asked her to meet him tomorrow at the Blue Heron at five o'clock for dinner. Relieved she would be seeing him again soon, Donna rested on the couch. Regardless where Eli might take her, Donna sensed she that she followed the correct path. The events of the past few days began to catch up with her. She quickly fell asleep on the couch, while imagining the next direction her life might take.

She dreamed she walked alone in a blinding snowstorm, trudging her way across the terrain into a wooded area. The sun had disappeared over the horizon, lightly masking the environment in twilight. Several men in dark clothing appeared from behind the thin alders and tried shooting her as she stumbled along the trail. The swirling snow blinded the shooters and lent protection. She raised her head and found Eli levitating in the air around her as if an apparition. Donna twirled around briefly in the falling snow trying to see him better, but he disappeared from her view. She looked down at her thick, heavy boots. The black shoes contrasted with the pale-blue tinted snow. Eli guided her to safety.

She found herself in a different place. Donna later dreamed she stood on the edge of the forest. The wooded area remotely reminded her of the company crew and hazardous waste site. In front of her, only two feet away, stood an icy slippery slope. Slowly, she made her way up the incline. Only a matter of time before her assailants found her again, she climbed to escape.

On a high ledge of the ice-covered, rocky mountain stood Eli. He called to her, lowering a red and blue-striped climbing rope to assist her. He leaned over the edge to be sure she could grab the rope. Covered in a dark hooded coat for protection from the elements, his face hid from her view, though she recognized his energy and form.

Awaking slowly, Donna slipped out of the dream, which faded away while she continued to climb the icy mountain in the snow. Fragments of the dream stirred in her memory, despite being too groggy to comprehend its entirety. Donna traversed the slippery slope with a lifeline from Eli. Being under duress, she had no place left to go but up, where Eli called her to safety.

After preparing a light dinner, Donna retired early. Immediately, she fell into a deep slumber, hibernating inside the womb of her subconscious until the early hours of a new day. She continued to follow the thread of the previous dream like the rope, which she had used to traverse the side of the mountain.

This time she found herself holding a rope that led to a yacht. A man reeled her towards the boat like a fish on a line, though he revered her like a mermaid. He appeared fascinated, yet anxious that he might lose his catch, a human that buoyed in the middle of the endless cape like a fish. The sunny blue sky hung over the water, saturating the surface with its warmth and promise. Small bright flags decorated the sails of the yacht, making the craft appear so cheerful and bright that Donna agreed to remain on the line. Not getting anywhere swimming alone in the cape, Donna watched herself eventually landed on deck. As both the catch and the witness, one self remained in the waves and observed the other's interaction with the man. The self that landed on deck embraced the man. Together, they turned and waved at the distant observer, still adrift and unattached in the waters.

Suddenly, a storm erupted over the cape and the skies became dark and cloudy. The rain fell on the sea so hard and fast that it was difficult to separate the water from the sky. The couple cast another line towards the witness, who caught it. They reeled her aboard as the thunder clapped and lightning zapped the sea. After boarding the yacht, the observer merged with the catch that remained arm-in-arm with the man on the boat.

Donna awoke the next day and remembered her last dream. She wrote it down in the journal that she kept by her bed. Then she calmly dressed for work and had some breakfast. Swiftly, she descended the stairs from her studio apartment, searching for the route that her friends took to the balcony.

At five o'clock sharp in the evening, Donna pushed aside the blue-shutter doors of the Blue Heron tavern. She spied Eli sitting at a table closer to the window at the far end of the restaurant. He rose to greet her, warmly taking her hand as he softly hugged and kissed her on the cheek. Donna brightened when she saw him and returned his affection without publicly calling attention to their blossoming love.

Together they slid into their chairs, conversed lightly, and quickly ordered. After a moment's pause Donna noticed Eli staring at her like the sailor of her dreams, a mixture of fascination, admiration, and anxiety that he might lose her. Donna slightly blushed, unaccustomed to the face in the mirror. He warmed her like the sun on a clear day over the waters of the cape.

The meal passed uneventfully. The couple glowed and basked in the delight of each other's company. Finally, Eli asked her, "Come with me to Washington D.C. next month. I have a meeting with the French ambassador."

Donna imagined the storm clouds coming. The voices in the restaurant and sounds from the street became thunderous. Lights in and outside the dimly lit restaurant seem to flicker. "Yes," she simply answered, as the weather became colder.

Chapter Nineteen

Did anyone on the planet ever sign up for a never-ending story?

Tune Reference: *Never Ending Story*

----Limahl

A MONTH LATER, Eli met Donna at the airport in Washington D.C.. She had caught the early flight from Boston and landed in Washington D.C. by seven o'clock in the morning. Carefully avoiding public displays of romantic affection, Eli softly kissed her hand and held it as he picked up her luggage with the other. Quietly, they walked out of the airport to a nearby shuttle. The shuttle took them to a small office park near the French Embassy, where Eli worked in a temporary office with colleagues.

When the shuttle dropped them off, Eli led Donna to a tiny office on the second floor. He invited her in the office and quickly closed the door behind them. Placing her bags on a shelf, he offered her a soft chair near the oak desk.

"Can I get you some tea?" he asked. "Our appointment with the Department for Nuclear Affairs is at nine o'clock."

Donna nodded, requesting a bagel with her cup of chamomile tea. She relaxed a little and regained her appetite. Eli asked the receptionist in the adjacent lobby to bring the refreshments. Returning his attention to her, he briefed Donna on the upcoming meeting.

Donna nodded, hearing his words. She remained deep in thought, considering all the angles and possibilities. Eli continued his monologue as he watched her silence. Only her eyes betrayed her thoughts. He felt encouraged by her contemplation and began to reflect on his own words, thinking through his analysis of the situation.

"I need another pair of eyes and ears," he said finally. Taking a deep breath, he looked at her directly. Rubbing his hands together in subtle anguish, he told her, "Thank you for listening. It helps to gather my thoughts before taking this bold stand. We could change the course of history in just fifteen minutes."

Tossing off the gravity of the moment, Donna glanced over his head and shrugged. With a light wave of her hand, she dismissed all his concerns as child's play. Then she looked at the clock and rose from her chair. Eli looked down and quickly began gathering his papers. After he finished packing, they left the building and walked next door.

At the embassy, Eli introduced Donna as his research assistant. The officer accepted her presence with a hearty handshake before he ushered them into his office. Shutting the door behind them, he motioned Donna and Eli toward some chairs. Donna sat down and glanced quickly at Eli. He appeared much more self-assured and confidant than his earlier delivery. She smiled slightly and faced the officer. With a wry grin, Eli glanced sideways in her direction. Assured that he had already won his case, he briefly presented the information. The officer listened intently and then addressed them.

"I looked over your documentation. Thank you very much." He confided, "It confirms what we have suspected."

Dropping his gaze from the couple, he continued as he looked out the window at the forest. He briefed them about the French Intelligence, created by De Gaulle following World War II. Over the past year, the service had been restructured and placed under the Department of Defense. The scandal involving the Moroccan revolutionary, Ben Barka, led the French government to this decision. Barka began his in exile in Paris during 1963, the same year of President Kennedy's assassination. Barka's presumed murder in 1965 indicated that France's intelligence network had been compromised.

"I understand that Jacqueline Kennedy sought help from the French after the assassination," Donna responded. "She had direct connections with the French secret intelligence from her parent's work during WWII."

"Yes, some claim that De Gaulle's French Intelligence published a book on the JFK assassination at Jackie's request. They claim that Bobby intended to use the publication for his presidential campaign. Bobby died shortly after the book surfaced in France."

"So, French Intelligence was compromised like the military forces in this country," Eli commented.

"This limited our country's effort with Jackie and Bobby," the French officer replied. "Now twenty years later we have rebuilt our intelligence agency. We are still in the process of rebuilding and gathering information. It will be at least fifteen years before we will be able to honor the Franco-American Alliance that Lafayette helped negotiate. We greatly appreciate the information you have given us."

"Barka's death alerted the French that their intelligence agency had been infiltrated," Donna surmised.

"Precisely," the officer answered.

Donna listened as Eli and the French representative discussed the details of the case. When they finished, the three of them amicably shook hands and promised to remain in close contact. The foundation for restoring the Franco-American Alliance from the American Revolution had been lain. Eli agreed to visit France and follow up on his investigation.

Eli and Donna left the embassy, returning to the tiny office. After dropping their book bags on the desk, they collapsed in the surrounding chairs and stared at the book bags. A few moments passed before their gaze fell from the objects to each other.

"How about a tour of the monuments and lunch before you leave this evening?" Eli ventured. "It will be a great way to center ourselves."

Donna agreed with a smile. Although her mood remained reflective mood from this morning's affairs, she abruptly began gathering her things.

"You can leave your bag here so that you don't have to carry it. We can get it on the way to the airport," Eli told Donna.

"That would be great," she replied pushing her bag aside.

Within minutes they were in a taxi headed for the National Mall. The taxi dropped them off at the Washington Monument, an obelisk towering 555-feet-high across the mall from the nation's Capitol. They obtained tickets and stood in line for the elevator that operated inside the obelisk. The elevator took them to the top of Washington Monument and provided a panoramic view of their surroundings. Commemorative stones, donated by various countries, states, and political parties to save construction costs, line the inside of the monument. Inscriptions on many of the stones could only be visible to those riding the elevator. Many of the engravings consisted of occult symbols or political agendas a step away from the life of George Washington.

"I doubt George Washington would have cared for this monument," Donna commented as they rode the elevator to the top. "The occult symbols on his dining room wallpaper at Mount Vernon consist of only the tools of his trade. He did not use symbols from ancient Egypt; he used plows and crops. He modeled himself as a Cincinnati rather than a phallic symbol."

Donna continued, "Washington served as the first president of the Society of Cincinnati established, after the American Revolution. They steered the country away from a military-industrial complex. The push to build this monument began in the early 1830's, about the time the royal illumined ones infiltrated the craft guilds and ran off with the Second National Bank. This occurred only thirty years after George Washington's death."

Donna paused briefly as the doors to the elevator opened. The view from the top of the monument offered a panoramic view of the National Mall. Eli and Donna slipped away from the crowd.

When they were out of eavesdropping range, Donna explained, "The French Jacobins supported the illumined ones, the same group that George Washington discussed in a letter to John Robison, a fellow occultist at Edinburg University. Robinson wrote *Proofs of a Conspiracy*, which nobody considered a theory. He supplied convincing proof for Washington."

Twenty-minutes after the elevator returned them to ground level, Eli and Donna exited and left the shadow of the monument. They walked over to the Jefferson Memorial as Donna elaborated, "The original name of this city was Rome, Maryland. They built it at a time when both Catholics and Protestants used the Romans for inspiration, regardless whether it was Cincinnati or Saint Peter's. The Capitol resembles a basilica. The Civil War erupted ten years after its expansion."

Eli took Donna's hand as they journeyed up the steps to the Jefferson Memorial, which resembled the Pantheon in Rome. Inside the memorial they found a statue of Thomas Jefferson carved in the manner of a robust god. They silently read the numerous quotes inscribed on the surrounding marble walls.

Donna read the one quote in the Jefferson Memorial that stood out from all the others. She repeated it out loud to Eli, "I have sworn upon the altar of God eternal hostility against every form of tyranny over the mind of man." Without looking up from the caption, Donna surmised, "Jefferson understood mind control. The quote is from a letter to Dr. Benjamin Rush, who was also known as the Father of American Psychology."

Perplexed, Eli looked around him for more information. Touring the National Monuments with a stratigrapher suddenly exposed historical patterns in astonishing simplicity. "Let's check out the FDR Memorial," he proposed, wondering what thread she would uncover next. They raced down the steps of the memorial and hurried towards the western edge of the Tidal Basin.

Soon Donna gave him an answer. After passing lightly through the rooms in the exhibit, she stopped suddenly in Room Three. The inscription came from a presentation given to a group of White House correspondents, shortly before Americans joined WWII. "Here's the most revealing line in the memorial," she told Eli. She read him the quote in a firm voice. "They (who) seek to establish systems of government based on the regimentation of all human beings by a handful of individual rulers call this a new order. It is not new and it is not order."

Not convinced, Eli stepped closer to the monument to read the caption.

"What a concept!" she announced, sarcastically waving her hands high in the air. "Both Woodrow Wilson and Churchill wanted to create a New World Order, whereas FDR equated it to something like a plague."

Eli stood silently beside Donna and reflected on the inscription. He began to connect the dots from his investigation. "One of the hypnotized witnesses that I had interviewed said that FDR had been assassinated," he admitted. "Stalin also thought that FDR had been poisoned. Cerebral aneurysms can be caused by drugs similar to rat poison."

Donna pulled Eli away from the FDR Memorial and quickly exited the exhibit. They hurried along the footpath to the edge of the Lincoln Memorial. Instead of visiting the rest of the memorials, they found solace in the Reflection Pool extending between the Washington Monument and Lincoln Memorial. They sat down on one of the park benches overlooking the water.

Eli interrupted the silence. He said facetiously, "I don't suppose that you'd want to visit the Albert Pike statue in front of the Judiciary. The National Parks Service honors him for his occultism and Confederate inclinations."

"I don't want to get into difficult-to-prove details of the Lincoln assassination, complete with Congressional smoke and mirrors." She repeated a popular quote, "As Lincoln said, 'A house divided cannot stand on its own.' Well, Lincoln had a house divided. The boys ran around in Confederate uniforms and teased the Union soldiers."

"I wonder who put them up to that."

"Maybe, the Union soldiers at the White House were confederate." Donna winked at Eli, before something across the mall caught her attention. Without hesitation, she suddenly rose from the bench. In a whisper, she suggested, "Let's skip the Lincoln Memorial too. We need to get out of here fast."

Perplexed, Eli watched her dash towards the street and hail a taxi. Pretending to not be associated with him, Donna talked to the driver in a voice loud enough so Eli could easily overhear. The taxi driver agreed to take her straight to the airport. Without time for explanations, Eli followed her cue and walked away as if they had never known each other. He eyed the group that had distracted Donna and wondered what had caused her flight. Something about the men with the black dog sent a shudder up his spine. He hopped the next shuttle back to the office.

Chapter Twenty

When you feel there's nothing left

Don't let go of what lies in front of you

And remember that you

Still have something to lead you through

Even if it is just a dream

Tune Reference: *Hold on Tight*

----Electric Light Orchestra

AFTER ELI ENTERED the small office nearby the French Embassy, he hurried to phone Dr. McClendon. "Can you have someone meet Donna at the Boston airport?" She saw someone she recognized and fled. We separated to avoid further danger," he told Dr. McClendon. "She left the mall in a taxi bound for the airport."

"Oh, no!" Dr. McClendon exclaimed. "I'll post two of her classmates at the Boston airport. We can track the arrivals from Washington D. C.."

When Donna arrived at the Boston airport, two men emerged from the crowd waiting for passengers to unload. They flanked her tightly on both sides and whisked her towards the building's exit. She smiled and brightened, recognizing them from her exercise class. They swept her away in one swift motion for the door. She glimpsed out of the corner of her eye and observed two men strategically placed in the crowd, watch her leave. From the view of an outsider, the two exercise brothers could have easily been mistaken for family members or boyfriends. As they whizzed past the shuttle driver waiting for customers near the building's exit, Donna noticed that the driver also seem to vaguely recognize her. She reassumed her *no-it-must-have-been-someone-else* air and tossed her head in the other direction as if she had never ever intended to take the shuttle to Woodsport. The appearance of the men did not escape the eye of one of her companions. Her classmate backed-off a couple of steps to see if someone followed them. Together the threesome hurried to a sports car parked a few hundred yards away and out of sight.

Without a word, Donna got into the car with her exercise brothers. The driver emerged from the airport parking lot and sped onto the highway towards the cape. The group remained silent for most of the trip as they monitored the road for signs of an attack. After parking the car a few blocks away from the apartment building, they escorted Donna to her apartment and checked it out for intruders. Satisfied that nothing had been disturbed, one of her exercise brothers handed a small red envelope to her. "I live three doors down if you need me. Michael lives in his girlfriend's apartment right underneath you on the first floor. Class is at seven o'clock this evening."

They left with a slight bow and grin, waving her off before she could give them gas money. Donna relented, noting their absolute refusal, and dropped her shoulders with a sigh. She expressed sincere gratitude. "Thank you."

After their departure, she brewed a cup of chamomile tea and sat down on the couch to read the letter from Eli. "Finishing loose ends here with the Embassy. Meet me at the beach in two days at 12:30 this afternoon. I'll bring lunch."

Donna tossed the red envelope in the air with delight. Later, that day Donna arrived at class and met Dr. McClendon in the hall. For the moment, they appeared the only ones in the room.

"Thank you for sending me the lifeline at the airport," Donna began. "I'm not sure I would have made it safely back to Woodsport otherwise."

"I know," Dr. McClendon replied. "Eli called and alerted me that you had fled the National Mall. Your classmates told me they saw a few shady characters hovering around the gate."

Donna swirled around and walked away. She glanced over her shoulder and smiled at Dr. McClendon. Stepping into the adjacent room, she dropped to the floor and began stretching. Dr. McClendon followed her in the room and practiced an exercise set. Donna told him, "Remember that leaflet you handed me a couple of months ago? I noticed a black dog on it."

"Yes, I recall that obtuse discussion about a black dog," Dr. McClendon said slowly as if carefully reeling in a prize fish.

Though she sensed he was pulling her in gently, she ignored the lure and persisted on her own accord. "The black dog is my friend Carrie's father. He is in deep, but tries to protect his daughter. She doesn't know it yet, but I do because of my awareness. His signal is the black dog symbol."

Dr. McClendon froze. Donna ignored him and persisted. "At first, I ran from the cue. I found it annoying, especially when I ran for my life. With time, I came to trust him and his team's communications."

Donna rose to her feet and stretched her hamstrings. "A group of men pursued a black dog on the National Mall. They seemed very conspicuous, purposely allowing the dog to run around. I would have thought nothing of it, but they were the same men I had seen near the beach. Eli and I must have been in very grave danger. The black dog doesn't usually come out of the shadows except for emergencies."

"Do you think you were tracked from the French Embassy?"

"No, we kept our guard. Somebody from the investigation must have recognized Eli on the National Mall. They probably did not know about the trip to the French Embassy."

Dr. McClendon nodded his understanding. Waving his hand in the air, he dismissed any further thoughts and conversation. He turned away and wiped his brow, indicating that he needed some time to reflect on this latest piece of information. Having locked the door behind Donna, he left to ushered in the group that had congregated outside. Without another word, he ducked into the office and silently brought her a cup of oolong tea.

Accepting his brew, Donna walked around the room to compose herself before class officially began. Her classmates happily greeted her again as they passed. Donna beamed at them, while quietly sipping her tea.

Two days later, she hiked the beach to the pile of logs where she had found Eli earlier. In his absence, she sat down on a log and stared out to sea. An entire year had been crammed into the past three months.

Hearing footsteps in the brush behind her, she turned to face the intruder. The surf pounded the shoreline and thunder echoed from distant clouds. A familiar voice greeted her from beyond the tall grass.

"Hi there!" Eli jubilantly shouted.

Donna jumped from the log. Eli ran down the path from her family cottage to the beach and hugged her. He lifted Donna in the air and twirled her around in his embrace. Eli let her down as she kissed him softly on the cheek. "You came down the path from my family's cottage."

"I know," he said. "Dr. McClendon told me about it sometime ago. I thought that I'd check on it. It appears vacant."

"I'll move back when this blows over," Donna stated. "My parents are too busy with other things to deal with this riff raff."

Eli sat down on a nearby log and started unpacking a picnic from his backpack. He motioned for Donna to sit down beside him. She complied and he handed her a tuna sandwich.

"I've missed you," Donna confessed. "Even though I've known you only for a few months, it feels like a lifetime."

"I want you to know that it has been an incredible lifetime," he continued. "I will be spending the next three months in France. I need to leave until the EPA's investigation gets under way, and the company has something else to worry about that is bigger than me." Then he knelt beside Donna on the log, and asked "Will you marry me when I return in three months?"

Donna nodded. "Yes."

Eli slipped a gold ring on her finger and kissed her.

Donna heard the crashing of the waves on the surf as the tide came in. She could feel his warmth as he moved closer until she fell suspended into a void. Eli pulled her in, only stopping when she felt an existential sense of safety. They lingered in this space for what seemed to be an eternal moment, both sensing the correctness of their decisions.

Chapter Twenty-One

Build bridges to connect

Rather than fortresses and embattlements

Tune Reference: *Fortress Around Your Heart*

----Sting

THREE MONTHS LATER, Eli whirled with Donna around the room as if in a long forgotten dream, during a moment so anachronistic that she could not believe she existed. Yet somehow she stood in the present, looking into the stillness of his blue eyes and enjoying his smile. She wore a full white bridal dress, as traditional as the image of a dancing cinderella and the king who found her. His simple stark-suit stood in contrast to the white, bringing a serene, modern, businesslike air to the waltzing couple. Only his starched-white silky shirt and pale bow tie complemented the feminine elegance held lightly in his arms.

He sipped champagne, between laughs and dances with his friends until the last few couples waved him off and left the wood floor of the studio. Life became his party. His cavorting had been broken only by interludes of silent joyful glances at the woman he married. The happy grin under his blonde mustache and shining eyes broadcasted the intensity of his serious devotion.

Once they found themselves alone, he took Donna by the hand and walked with her to a small cottage at the base of the nearby waterfall. The roar of the water silenced them on the few steps of the small porch. They kissed in the moist air of the night that enveloped them in a dark dancing swirl. Transformed from the lightness of the spray, he unlocked the wood-frame door with the oval-crystal window in the center and ushered her in.

He noticed the hint of resignation in her arm that had dropped to her side. She led him to the bedroom adjacent the living area. Though Donna loved and admired him, she seemed distracted. Like the dance that had taken place hours ago, they twirled in a whirlwind romance beset by circumstances so rapid and deep that it was all they could do to ride the tide and stay afloat. He softly kissed her lips as he rolled the short sleeve of her gown down to her side.

Eli stopped abruptly when her back tensed. Reaching into his left pocket, he presented her with a small red glass candleholder. Etched in the shape of a peaceful dove, the object refracted light through crystalline wings.

"You fixed it!" she exclaimed. Donna sighed as she cradled the candleholder in her hands and softly kissed his cheek. Tears came to her eyes and their happy blueness glistened.

Transfixed by the sincere expression of gratitude, Eli nodded his understanding. "Found another like the one Carrie bought."

He smiled, sensing that he had eased the tension. She placed the dove on the bedside table and fully embraced him, while still keeping up the momentum. The embrace became more fervent.

He explained earnestly, "I don't want this to be a jarring experience." Slowly and deliberately, he kissed her. Her fingers found the mark over his heart. A stray bullet had almost been fatal. For a moment her breathing stopped, then it became faster and faster. She sensed that he listened to his own rhythm, following his own drummer.

Lowering his head over her chest, he listened. His steely-grey blue eyes remained quiet. She felt the blood pulsing through his arms as he stilled. For a moment she felt suspended in endless time. Then he ran his hands around her breasts and down her body. He opened her like a flower, kissing and inhaling her simultaneously. She felt a sense of grace that someone finds when opening a flower or escaping a fatal wound. Like the scarlet dove resting on the table nearby, the peaceful sensation nested her.

She listened to his shallow breathing and felt his heart pound over her. Feeling the strength of his gentle, inquisitive rhythm, she trembled subtly. Standing in the deep dark recesses of their joined minds, a wave emerged from the depth and carried them to separate shores. Together they lingered in this dream state for a small eternity, rolling with the waves as they appeared. They heard the pounding of the nearby waterfall in their ears and smelled the mist in the air. The intensity of the sound built suddenly as they heard the water spilling beyond the barriers and rocks lying at the depths. What appeared motionless at the surface continued to flow at the deeper levels.

Falling asleep in the warmth of their intertwined bodies, he softly whispered, "I love you," before succumbing to the drifting current inside him.

She echoed his words while he still heard her. They quieted for several hours and awoke later in the vague dawn. Finding him again, she pulled him gently towards her. Donna's hands groped over the contours of his chest as her hands slid behind his neck. Eli tucked his chin in the crevasse beneath her ear and slowly inhaled her essence until she seemed fully aroused. Then she stopped suddenly as her head shook from one side to another. Her breathing grew heavy.

Pausing for a brief moment, he rolled around and placed her over him so that he could get a better look. Her eyes remained shut; he felt her shake. A small tear escaped from the corner of an eyelid. His eyes blinked until they fully opened and he kissed the salty drop that had spilled. Feeling her withdraw into a remote world, he held her tight against his body.

Donna responded and ran her lips over him. Remaining lost in a world beyond, she tasted his sweetness as if it was the only way she knew he was there. Once satisfied she still had him before her, she uncovered him and slightly opened her eyes to behold him. Eli caught her in the air and joined her consciousness, happy that she had awoken.

Chapter Twenty-Two

Sometimes pain exists

To prevent excess

Tune Reference: *Home*

----Daughtry

REGAINING CONSCIOUSNESS IN the twilight, Eli turned towards the motionless woman beside him. He watched her for any signs of apprehension, soon becoming entranced by her serenity. Donna's chest heaved with each wispy breath, exposing a fragile life force that compelled him to put his arm around her to secure her frame. Wishing to touch her throughout eternity, he felt the magic of this wild, rhythmic beating heart beside him. Inspired by her, Eli imagined the possibilities of their lives together.

Donna awoke from the depth of this haze to the sound of the nearby waterfall, as the moisture of the spray lingered in the air around her. The events of the previous night brought her full circle, where time and the plunging waters erased the jagged edges of her memory. There had been so much to learn, she thought, fingering the scar on her lover's chest as a warm tear escaped her right eye.

Donna rolled over on her back and stared at the wooden ceiling. She felt renewed as if the waters of life had freed her soul of any misgivings it may have had for the fork in the road she had taken. She gazed at the scarlet peace dove that Eli had given her as a wedding present. Where would it go now?

"It's OK," Eli whispered. "We own this place. We don't have to leave. You're home."

More tears flooded Donna's eyes. She wiped them automatically away, but more came. The young woman buried her head over his chest as her heart raced. His long outstretched arm drew inwards and wrapped around her.

"I signed the papers last week," he told her.

Donna sighed with relief. Protective space had become important to her over the past several years. Her heart calmed down.

Softly unraveling from his arms, Donna rose and walked to the window overlooking the base of the waterfall. Wanting to be in her own space again, she gazed quietly at the fast-flowing current that never stopped. If every drop of water represented an increment in time, then the continual flow carried only whatever had a lighter density. Once in the white-water rapids, there remained no time to collect baggage. Her nude silhouette stood silently behind the white lace curtains as she reflected on the course before her.

Eli grinned happily as he studied the figure at the window. He left the bed to join her. Being careful to avoid disturbing her thoughts, he touched her through the lace. The man deftly unhooked the curtain with one long arm and veiled the curtain around her body. Donna closed her eyes as he drew near. Allowing him to sweep her in his arms, she did not refuse his entrance. When he felt her body collapse into silence, he carried her across the room and settled in an adjacent rocking chair. Cuddling the woman in his arms, he slowly rocked as her head fell across his shoulder. Then he kissed her tenderly on the cheek.

"You only had tens of thousands of people who wanted to kill you," he broke it to her in hushed voice. "Almost as many involved in the Lincoln assassination."

Into reality therapy, Eli paradoxically stripped away any illusions between them as he covered her body with the curtain. Donna felt the stirring of his desire for her and it unnerved her.

"It helped to get the Last Rites," she ruefully observed. The notion of incurring the wrath of thousands of people troubled her. "It will be the last time I worry about the pope at a catholic college, especially one operated by self-confessed confederates. I thought the confederacy thing was an antiquated, royal economics program."

Pausing briefly, she wiggled a little in his arms as she added, "Little did I know that occult terrorists disliked Pope John the 23rd. Little did I know that occult terrorists held honored status at the university. Little did I know that the ex-premier of Hungary surfaced at Dealey Plaza. Little did I know that the Warren Commission questioned the former president of the college. Little did I know that most of the economics professors were sponsored by Mises...Connect those dots..."

"Enough...shh..." Eli softly told her as he seemingly lifted her troubles away. He touched her silent wounds and soothed her until the angst transformed her body. Comforting her like a small child, Eli continued to rock her gently.

Relieved, Donna kissed him without further words. Their heartfelt embrace became more passionate, resuming their lovemaking in the sunbeam emanating from behind the bellowing window curtains. Eli held her tightly in his arms as she swung around him. He leaned back as she plunged herself into him. The chair rocked behind him and then abruptly rebounded with new life.

"We have an edge," he whispered to Donna. "I can stop you from going over. You can be brought back when you go beyond the veil." Fervently, he pulled her closer to him, running his hands over her breasts and torso until he found her again. Once satisfied, he spoke softly in her ear, "Imagine our lives together. We're a wildcard."

Remaining quiet, Donna threw herself into him again. She felt him expire senseless in the light-filled void of endless time. Content that she had caught him in free fall, Donna allowed him to find her in suspended space. They met halfway, giving and taking until they lost track of the moment.

"We'll bring back the MidEarth," Donna responded, quietly in their state of being. "We need to remember ourselves, and come to terms with the loss we fear the most."

"MidEarth?" he asked. "Where?"

"Right underneath us," she murmured. "I sense that our friends from the wedding have found it by now."

"How did you suspect?" he questioned, aroused.

She gasped, her head falling over his shoulder. Their bodies shook uncontrollably as rocking chair stilled with the gravity of their interaction. In a hushed voice, she confided, "I saw it in the spray of the waterfall. A rainbow appeared in the mists."

Eli shut his eyes and lowered his head between her breasts. He whispered, "I love you."

She leaned away from him. Eli held her securely. Tenderly looking at him in the eye, she responded, "I love you. Together we can make it so that the next generation doesn't have to run. They will grow up knowing the earth, the sky, and the MidEarth with all its inspiration and wonders."

"Make it safe to love," Eli added. "Heal ourselves. Be free to dream and learn."

Donna threw her arms around him with a smile. Feeling content, he gently stroked her back as he felt her heave several full breaths. Within the other they found a safe harbor and stayed there for the rest of their lives. After a brief pause, Eli carried her to bed where they drifted into sleep, awaking several hours later to see the light of day.